ALSO BY NETTIE JONES

Mischief Makers

FISH TALES

FISH TALES

A NOVEL

Nettie Jones

FARRAR, STRAUS AND GIROUX   NEW YORK

Farrar, Straus and Giroux
120 Broadway, New York 10271

Copyright © 1983, 2025 by Nettie Jones
Afterword copyright © 2025 by Nettie Jones
All rights reserved
Printed in the United States of America
Originally published in 1984 by Random House
First Farrar, Straus and Giroux hardcover edition, 2025

Library of Congress Cataloging-in-Publication Data
Names: Jones, Nettie, author.
Title: Fish tales : a novel / Nettie Jones.
Description: First Farrar, Straus and Giroux hardcover edition. |
    New York : Farrar, Straus and Giroux, 2025.
Identifiers: LCCN 2024038333 | ISBN 9780374608804 (hardcover)
Subjects: LCGFT: Erotic fiction. | Novels.
Classification: LCC PS3560.O5235 F5 2025 | DDC 813/.54—
    dc23/eng/20240819
LC record available at https://lccn.loc.gov/2024038333

Designed by Abby Kagan

Our books may be purchased in bulk for promotional, educational, or
business use. Please contact your local bookseller or the Macmillan
Corporate and Premium Sales Department at 1-800-221-7945, extension
5442, or by email at MacmillanSpecialMarkets@macmillan.com.

www.fsgbooks.com
Follow us on social media at @fsgbooks

1   3   5   7   9   10   8   6   4   2

To my daughter, Lynne C. Harris

The human fish is intricate and hidden; the appearance of his fins are deceptive.

—JEAN TOOMER, *Essentials*

FISH TALES

PROLOGUE

Mrs. Annie Simmons strutted down her front porch steps one May day butt-naked except for a pair of high-heeled pink satin bedroom slippers and a short strand of coral-colored pop beads. I was walking down her side of the block on my way home from school for lunch. She paused at the top of her steps, looked like she was listening for the music. When she heard it, she clapped her hands, smiled, kicked up first one leg and then the other, and began swaying her hips from side to side. Then she kicked high again. Her scraggy breasts swayed as she slowly switched down those steps, kick, sway, switch forward. Kinky red hairs covered her private parts. When she reached the bottom step, she threw her arms out, clapped again, snapped her fingers, shook her head, and began her routine again. Kick! Sway! Switch forward!

When she got out to the edge of the sidewalk, she turned around and faced her house, bent over from her waist, and started playing with herself. Just as this seemed to get good to her, a black police truck came skidding around the corner. Two blond policemen jumped out of the truck and Mr. Simmons came out of the house, crying, carrying a patchwork quilt. His wife was squatting dog fashion, touching herself, when they ran up and knocked her down on her back. Mr. Simmons threw the quilt over her head. Then he jumped on top of her, holding her down. I could hear him say, "Oh, Annie! Baby! My po' baby! What's wrong, Annie?" Those are the first words I ever remember hearing Mr. Simmons say to anyone other than "Good day." Mrs. Simmons didn't say anything. She just lay there looking up at the sky, snot running from her nose, thick spit formed at the corners of her mouth. As they went to pick her up, she looked at them only long enough to spit in Mr. Simmons's face. After that she just closed her eyes, seemed to be asleep.

PART ONE

DISCONNECT

JASON STEEL

J ason had a crooked smile and he had a crooked way, called himself Pasqua because he thought his father was part Mexican. Proudly he had said, "I'm part Mexican, part Irish, part Chinese, part Spanish, part Indian, and part Negro." In what order and what proportions? That's what I had thought, looking at the long, skinny, shit-yellow boy of twenty that lay beside me grinning. We were in his vacationing sister's bed. Jason was as pleased with his sis as he was with his international heritage. She was part Jewish, I learned in time. He was trying to kiss me. I was pretending not to know how to French kiss. See, Jason's teeth were not only yellow. The ones left were decayed, too; little black ant-size specks sat on his front ones. He had a wide gap and true to the old folks' saying he lied a lot. I didn't like lying on his sister's bed with him and I didn't like him. But I had to do whatever he wanted, I thought, because of my condition. I'd missed a period and at sixteen that usually does not indicate menopause. I was scared of not obeying him, his knowing I didn't like him. I closed my eyes as he pushed back Sis's white satin quilted comforter and sheet. I didn't want to see his great big thing ever again. Nor did I wish to look as he pulled my half-slip up and my drawers off. In the early fifties good girls didn't look. They surely didn't undress themselves for any boy. I bet you my mama never did.

"What a pretty body you have," he said as he eased my white cotton drawers down my legs and off my feet. I really don't know if Jason was lying or not, because I think I was twenty-five before I ever dared look at my body carefully enough to appraise it. I didn't look at my own asshole until I was thirty-three. I was hoping Jason wouldn't look at my big feet as he pulled my panties over them. I hated my toes; the first two were as long as my big one. I'd also developed corns by sixteen from trying to stuff size tens into size eight and a half. Jackie Kennedy did more for me in the sixties than anyone when they printed the size of her feet in the Detroit *Free Press* that time. Jason had really small feet for a man six foot three. I'd say size ten, wide instep, short toes, and a nicely rounded heel. His spindly legs looked better covered, however; they were perfectly straight and hairless. He didn't look at my feet at all; he was too busy trying to get into me. The grease in his Quo Vadis haircut felt nasty on my belly as he kissed it, making smacking sounds as he traveled down my "pretty body."

I tried as best I could to hold my thighs together when he got to that part. I opened my eyes up just long enough to focus on Sis's gold ceiling. My, how I hoped he'd skip the fingering procedure. I hated his sticking his finger aimlessly in and out of my body. All it did was agitate me. I turned my face slowly into the pillow. I didn't want him to see the undiluted disgust in my eyes. "Are you ready?" he asked hoarsely as he slinked up my body. I tried to relax 'cause I knew that the moment he felt his thing on my thing he was going to ram me for all he was worth. Jason, like so many men I have known since, loved dramatic entrances. Maybe, I thought as he swiveled his hips into motion, if I help him hurt me, I'll lose the baby. I won't have to tell anyone.

"That's it, Lewis, give it to me. Whew! It feels so good. You like it, don't you? I can tell you do," he said breathlessly on a backswing. "You been acting like you didn't like it." He was slamming it now. Sweat was dripping down my thighs, making squeaky sounds. In one fell swoop, he had my legs up and over his shoulders. He was really ready to dig into me now. I scooted unashamedly up on his narrow, hairless yellow chest, spreading my thighs as wide as I could. I tried to swallow him, I thought I felt the blood.

"I think I feel blood," I said. "I don't want to get any on your sister's pretty white sheets."

In the bathroom, I frantically unrolled some toilet tissue and wedged it between my legs. No blood, just that snot.

Holding one of his beloved sister's fluffy yellow monogrammed towels around my body, I returned to that room and crept back into that woman's bed beside him. He was lying there with the covers still thrown back, twirling a strand of his hair with his fingers, drinking a glass of Kool-Aid and watching an old Alan Ladd film. I waited until the commercial break before I broke the news. "I'm pregnant. About two months, I think," I said delicately, looking right at his face for the first time in a long time, it seemed.

He grinned slyly as he resumed watching that commercial. "Pregnant? Whose baby? Anyone I know?"

Jason and eight of his friends pulled a train on a girl one time. They belong to this elite club called the Quadrilles. Jason was the president and founder; twelve of the members participated in this project. I'm sure the only reason I wasn't invited was that Jason wasn't being seen with me because of my prenatal condition (we talked on the telephone when everyone else at our houses was asleep).

One of the girls smelled a rat when she saw nine-to-two odds at the party. She sneaked out the back door on her way from the toilet, I heard, without mentioning her move to the other girl. Jason and the boys got this one drunk on Sneaky Petes. Then he took her to Sis's room and showed her how much he loved her. I heard that after he finished showing her they all came in and took turns showing her how loved she was by them.

That girl was secretly hospitalized by her mother the next day in a state of hysteria. She nor her mother ever told on Jason and his friends. They were too ashamed.

J ason," I whispered into the phone late one night. "We don't have to get married now. My mother took me to this abortionist a friend of hers told her about. She said it was almost too late but she'd try. Everything's gonna be all right again," I said, looking down at my swollen stomach. "She said it'll probably happen tonight."

"How'd she do it?" he asked.

"With a hanger," I whispered back.

PETER BROWN

My white bobby socks were dusty from the gravel of the playground by the time I got to my eighth-grade social studies class the first day of school. Mud streaked the white part of my saddle oxfords. My new social studies teacher's black penny loafers almost threw off a reflection of the room, they were so shiny. He was standing at the hallway door talking to Mrs. Hiller and Miss Weinstein. Mrs. Hiller kept running her hands through her long wavy hair. Miss Weinstein didn't touch herself; she kept touching his arm where his starched white shirt was folded back. Every now and then they would all laugh. To me, his laughter sounded the way clear golden apple cider looks.

That first day he had us make a circle around him, and

then he read poetry to us. Robert Frost: "But I have prom-
ises to keep, and miles to go before I sleep." I thought
Mr. Brown was reading to me because whenever I looked
at him he was looking at me with this smile in his eyes.
Betty Washington swore when we were playing on the
playground that he was reading to her. She could tell,
she said, because whenever she looked up at him he was
looking at her titties. She had the biggest in class. My
grandmother told my mother, when she thought I didn't
hear, that Betty Washington was probably letting boys
feel on her and that's why she was so big. Mr. Brown
made Betty his book-room captain.

One Tuesday afternoon, right before Christmas, as I
left Pauline's Beauty Shop, I saw Mr. Brown let Betty out
of his car in front of her house. She had a J. L. Hudson's
shopping bag with a big box wrapped in gold paper and
green ribbon. She didn't see me. But he did as he slowly
turned his new black Mercury around. Quite naturally,
I waved. As he drove up to the curb in front of me, he
reached over and opened the door. I got in and stepped
on Betty's angora cardigan sweater, which was on the
floor of the car. The seat was warm. He didn't say anything except "Hi." He just started driving slowly down
Mt. Elliot, in the opposite direction from my house. He
didn't stop until we got to Belle Isle. I didn't say anything
when he put his hand on my knee. He kept his other

hand on the steering wheel and looked straight ahead. I don't think I was breathing when he turned in his seat and slid his hand up to where Walter, the boy across the street, used to try to touch when we'd all play doctor on his back porch. Mr. Brown sighed and pushed his tongue between his lips as he pushed the leg of my white cotton pants aside. I closed my eyes tight when he started rubbing and squeezing me down there. He started talking in this soft little voice. "I wanna see," he whispered, placing his head under my skirt, lifting it just a little. "Like the silk fuzz on a baby's head," he whispered. I squeezed my eyes tighter. I must have squeezed my legs, too, because he took his hands and reopened them. When he started kissing me there, the tears just slid from behind my eyes. At about the same time I opened my eyes and sneaked a look at his face because it felt like I was peeing.

OHoly Night" was the song the church organist was quietly playing in the background as I waited for Peter Brown's second wedding ceremony, Saturday, the night before Christmas 1962. My new friend Woody and I sat right by the door where Peter would enter with his best man. I'd graciously arranged this seating. I wanted my pretty, smiling face to be the one to greet him as he came into the church. I'd demurely pulled the sheer gold veil back on my pillbox hat so that he could see me clearly. The guests around us whispered in the kinds of tones used at a funeral about how lovely she'd arranged everything. "She's having a society band that usually only plays in Grosse Pointe at the reception.

They're going to Ocho Rios for their honeymoon. She's so lucky." I was trying to decide if I should object when that old piece of bullshit about anyone objecting came up during the ceremony. I was happy that Woody looked so rich sitting next to me. I was hoping that Peter would freak when he saw the almost topless gold beaded dress I wore under Sestra's autumn haze mink coat. I planned on his seeing it in the moment before I walked up to him in the reception line and planted a real kiss on his face. I could still feel the scratch marks between my thighs where Peter's head had lain only four hours ago.

"Here he is," I said to no one in my excitement as the vestibule door opened and Peter sallied out to what I thought was the tune of "O Little Town of Bethlehem."

"That's Peter, my degenerate schoolteacher," I said to Woody as Peter flashed a toothy grin at me. "Doesn't he look beautiful?" I whispered as I looked at Peter's back.

"That tuxedo makes him look like a waiter to me," Woody whispered, placing his long arm around my shoulders.

Sestra says it takes twelve hours for a man his age to regenerate, I thought as the organist began to play the "Wedding March." I saw myself standing over their bed this morning, crying, drunk from the bottle of champagne we consumed before we made love, heard myself all over again ask Peter, "Why her?" I heard him answer all over again in his girlish voice as he lay there naked, curled up like a snake looking up at me, "She understands me."

T hat son of a bitch," I whispered as I ran up his apartment steps still damp from his body. "I was twelve years old. He was twenty-six. Jesus Christ, he has been fuckin' me around since I was twelve. I wasn't even paying full fare at the movies when he molested me." I was running up those steps, crying. My breathing was beginning to take on that animal sound. I couldn't close my mouth for the breathing. My eyes hurt from the stretching the anger was causing.

"What do you want, Lewis?" a shirtless him asked, blocking my way to his apartment. "Jodi is sleeping. I'll talk to you later," he promised, whispering, as I tried to push past him.

"What do you want, Lewis?" Jodi called out from their bedroom. "Come on in, I'm just getting up," she said in a hoarse South Florida drawl.

Breaking his hold, I rushed past him into her trap. Jodi was lying on their brass king-size bed, nude, smoking a Turkish-smelling cigarette. "Here, catch one of my smoke rings," she said, directing a perfect ring toward me. For forty-three she was pretty well kept. Her short olive legs were slightly spread.

"She's really crazy this morning, baby," he said, standing in the doorway.

"Crazy," I said as I grabbed his head, slamming my fists into it. We must have looked like those Apache dancers as he held on to me. Exasperated by our embrace, I went limp in his arms long enough for him to let go. When he did, I raised my head, cleared my throat, and spit into his face. I hit right between his forehead and his nose. His look of innocent surprise lasted only a moment. When he started toward me, she yelled out, "Don't do it, Pete. She's kicked her own ass."

Looking first at her and then me like a confused young child, he asked, "What's wrong with you, Lewis? I've been honest with you. I thought you understood." Then he slowly turned and walked out, leaving the two of us alone. I wanted to beg him to stay and tell her that he loved me. "Tell her that you have always loved me, bastard" leaped out of me. "Desecrator, rapist, slimy child molester" spilled out of me into that quiet room.

"Pete told me you were nuts," she said from her bed. "He was right. He told me that he's tried to help you since you were twelve."

"Help me?" I screamed out. "By fucking me? Huh?"

"Most men believe that their dicks are better than penicillin," she said, sliding under the covers. "Lewis, I'm real sleepy," she drawled. "Why don't you go on home, talk to your daddy. Perhaps he'll explain that pussy is nothing to most old men nowadays. It ain't sacred anymore. It ain't even scarce. Wake up, Lewis, try giving some money instead, or understanding. Give something that is rare."

I was trembling now with embarrassment. "Is that what you offered him?"

"Precisely," she said. "I used my head. Peter can have all of the poon he can get for cocktails and lies. You, my dear, have lost a good lover today and an old friend. He did care for you. Disconnect your brain from your pussy, girl," she said, lazily turning over in their bed, feigning sleep.

"How old were you when you disconnected?"

"Oh, about thirty-five," she whispered drowsily.

"I'm only thirty-two," I said. "Thanks for the tip.

Now I can spend an extra three years as a hard, bitter old woman," I said, walking out of her bedroom.

"Not hard and bitter, Lewis, perhaps peaceful and sweet."

"I prefer to stay plugged in, Jodi. Plugged in makes me feel alive," I shouted as I slammed their apartment door.

WOODY

he first time I saw Woody he was standing at
Peter Brown's bar watching Peter's guests dance.
I noticed him because he kept this smile on his
face all the time. It took me years to understand that a
smiling face does not always indicate happiness. He had
come in with two women: Peaches and Isadora. Peaches
shot herself after her fifth husband kicked her down a
flight of steps. Isadora settled in New York and disappeared. Someone said they saw her getting in a big limousine one day around Gramercy Park, looking every bit
the grand lady. She didn't speak. Rumor has it she was
passing.

By the time Peter put on the slow music and lowered
the lights, I'd forgotten Woody. I was too drunk to do

anything but stare at my man Peter, dancing with his woman Jodi. I really thought I'd pass out. Peter was my entire life. He had been since I was twelve.

Jodi was doing The Run-Around at a frantic pace. Peter was doing The Pony. Her long curly hair nearly brushed me in the face, we were so close. I wanted to lock my hands in her hair and pull it until her neck snapped. To get away from my feelings, I turned to Woody.

"Got a light?" I asked, with my cigarette dangling from my lips.

"I sure don't," he responded, just grinning the way I mentioned. "You really smoke a lot."

"You've been watching me?"

"Sure have," he responded, taking a sip from his drink. "I've been watching you watch them," he said as he nodded toward Peter and Jodi. Peter's hand was cupping her ass right at the crack. Their eyes were closed. "Your face is very honest. I like that," he said, smiling as usual.

I asked Woody to marry me right after he happily consented to wait in my bedroom closet when Peter visited me unexpectedly. Peter always just dropped by. My home was his home sort of thing. This particular Sunday he dropped by while Jodi attended noon mass. I knew he

wanted a little piece the moment I saw the brown paper bag wrapped around the pint of gin. Gin was always
served before sex. This time it was against the kitchen
wall, as quietly as possible.

Promptly at twelve-thirty a satisfied Peter left to pick
up his wife. And I went to let Woody out of the closet.
There he sat, on top of my shoes, smiling. I proposed
right then, right there. And he accepted right then, right
there. Seems no one had ever asked him before. He was
truly flattered.

We married three months later on Peter Brown's first
wedding anniversary. Peter didn't RSVP and he didn't
come.

One morning after I got out of an overnight stay in jail for charges of malicious damage to property over a hundred dollars, Sestra drew this conclusion: "Woody has the most fascinating personality for a man. Now, it is true that you broke out Robin Lexington's picture window and climbed through it. Isn't it?"

"True," I admitted, noting new brown specks in her eyes.

"You did try to attack Robin with his own fireplace poker after you got in. Right?"

"Sure did," I responded, taking a cigarette out of her pack.

"Then Woody went over to Robin's house and sat him

down and told him that he'd scored ninety-nine percent several times on the artillery range. Right?"

"Right!" I blew my first smoke ring as she stared in amazement at me.

"That's when Robin decided to drop the charge?"

"Right!"

"Fascinating," Sestra responded, trying to blow one, too.

feel so much better being with you," Woody said ever so gently in the dark. "I rest better when I'm with you. I do love you." At this, he got out of the bed and turned his favorite Andrés Segovia record over. Woody was a freak for guitar players. He sounded like he'd been sleeping a long time, too. I could hear the evening traffic subsiding outside on Waverly Place. It must have been very late.

"How long," I asked, "have I been out?"

"Three days, baby." He walked over to the small refrigerator in my room and got out a beer as he talked.

"I got any Valiums left?"

"A few."

"Any champagne?"

"An entire bottle. I bought it while I was out. Like my new Segovia?"

I flashed back on that night-duty nurse blocking that elevator at St. Vincent's. "She has to wait for her doctor," she'd said. "She's not well."

"I am her doctor," Woody had said, reaching over her shoulder to push the button.

After he'd sprung me we stopped at the Lion's Head for a drink. I hadn't gotten beyond the second martini before the bar became all lights to me.

"Gimme a Valium. I'll drink the champagne and tell you what happened when I wake up," I promised, remembering sitting on Augus's loft steps, chipping at my wrists with a broken champagne glass.

KITTY

I soaked in Mother Bracey's Relaxo Bath Minerals until the skin on my feet looked a thousand years old. Then I water-picked my teeth until my gums were rosy. For a minute I thought about checking out the hotel's cafeteria, but nobody interesting would be there on Christmas evening who didn't feel much the same as I did, unless he was a Muslim. I didn't want to spend Christmas evening with any little old lady either. Too much like looking into a living crystal ball. Absentmindedly I reached into the robe pocket and pulled out a gold embossed business card. "Dial Your Desire," it advertised. Listed were two numbers. Turning it over I recognized Augus's handwriting. "Kitty," it said. Without hesitating I grabbed the telephone and dialed the number. The bastard, I thought. "So that's the 'work' he had to do on Christmas night." Tears of rage, frustration, and self-pity streamed as I lit a cigarette and waited for her to answer. "Seven, five, six, one," a high-pitched male voice uttered. "What's your desire?"

Without even thinking, I responded, "I want two men making love to me. My Christmas present to me."

"This is a holiday night, Puddin'. I'll have to come myself. Most of my boys have disappeared on me. I'll see what I can do." So have mine, I thought.

"Are you familiar with our rates? All righty, then," he went on immediately. "One hour of what you want will cost two hundred and fifty dollars. We accept cash only . . . I'm not far from your hotel, Boobee," he commented when I gave him my address. "Soon as I get dressed and pick up the other half, I'll be there."

Hanging up, I immediately began to pull the hotel sheets off the bed. Two hundred and fifty dollars made this a very special occasion. Within ten minutes I'd dressed the bed in my personal set of pink sheets trimmed with antique white lace and sprayed with wild-thyme perfume. My wisteria-scented candles were ablaze on the dresser just seconds afterward. Passing the vanity mirror, I decided to take off the hotel's white terry cloth robe. For this my finest: the pink and blue satin kimono Woody sent me last Christmas. I'd worn it once, for Augus, last spring before I'd left for Jamaica to avoid investing in his summer project—wholesaling a cargo of hair straightener to Nigeria. After he removed my kimono, he hung around my waist the long strand of pearls I always wore. My navel quivered even now, remembering where he'd started loving me. Never once had he mentioned my departure. All he'd said was he'd probably have less time in his schedule for me in the spring.

Nervously I turned the radio knob until I found the right music. Kenny Burrell filled the room with "Merry Christmas, Baby." Rushing to the bathroom, I put on light makeup, striving for a youthful, dewy effect. The doorbell rang just as I finished dotting my pulse points with a little fragrance of dianthus. I was into smelling like herbs at the time.

Breathing deeply, three times, I opened the door. There stood the most beautiful man I'd ever seen at any door of mine. He was wearing a cocoa-brown coat that belted around his tiny waist. A long white silk scarf hung casually around his neck. His skin was tan, almost the color of his coat. "Hi, Princess," he said, placing a bottle of Cristal champagne into my hands. Long eyelashes fluttered a time or two before he continued. "Couldn't find a proper partner, but I came over anyway. I seldom get a call from a lay-di! May I come in?" he asked as I backed up to let him pass. "I liked your address, too. I'll give you a fifty percent discount and stay for the evening if you like. It is Christmas and we're both alone." He unbuttoned his coat as he talked, surveyed my room. "Smells like my grandmother's house on Christmas. All we're missing is the lights. Wanna work on that?" he asked, grinning, taking off his scarf. "I'm Kitty, Princess. You have a second desire?" With this he dropped his blue jeans, which were all he had on underneath that coat, and turned slowly so that I could decide.

When I looked up, I was dancing on the edge of the floor with this little olive girl. Twirling colored lights cascaded from the high ceiling, making me feel like heaving up my Manhattans. She was focused on my mouth, smiling, snaking her hips to the music. Now and then she'd smack her gum to the beat. I must have looked like a version of those Midwestern businessmen having a night out on the town. I heard the sounds but I just couldn't connect with the beat. All around me dancers were writhing to the beat, lost in the music. Boys danced with boys, boys danced with girls, girls danced with anyone. It was rumored that Diana and Liza had been there earlier. Their electricity remained. A female disc jockey wearing a plastic jumpsuit with plastic rhinestoned studs, for courtesy, worked in the glass-enclosed cage above our heads. When she went into reggae, Jimmy Cliff, my girl reached up and placed her hands around my waist to help me with the beat. When I didn't resist, she slinked on up to my breasts, cupping them, still gyrating, pumping. Just as she placed her thumb and index fingertips on my nipples, Kitty came galloping up. Shaking the perspiration out of his freshly straightened and dyed mane, he grabbed me from behind. With the passion he reserved for hooking, he began to work on my neck and behind. I hoped they'd stop before I fainted. I heard Martha and the Vandellas' "Heat Wave" come on as the oldie-but-goodie selection. I remembered it from the summer I'd asked Woody to marry me . . . "Just a raging in my soul," Kitty blared in my ear.

A wakening in my bed between Kitty and my dance partner, I blushed. Her lips were pressed against my cheek. Kitty had his behind pressed against my belly. "Morning, Puddings. How are my angels?" He sounded like a regular man.

"I feel like the meat in a sandwich," I replied as she squeezed up behind me.

"Prime," she uttered. "I've got to split, playmates!" She must have felt my discomfort. Turning over, she reached for her panties as she talked. Her legs were long for her height. Slowly she slid into this pair of flesh-colored lace. Standing, she squeezed her crotch and sighed, "You two! Wow!" Strands of kinky hairs strained to get out of her drawers. Picking up her white pantsuit off our chair, she glided into our bathroom. We pretended we were asleep as she dressed.

"We loved it, Buster," Kitty purred when she reentered the room. "Give us a ring. Me lady and I are out whenever the moon is full. If I don't feed her, I have to chain her to this bed." I blushed, remembering the night.

"I'll teach you to dance," she promised, bending down to kiss me. I kept my eyes closed as she talked. I wanted her to go.

"She's asleep, Doll," Kitty said, rising. He knew I was feeling mean. "Give us a call," he repeated.

"Surely," she said, letting go of me. "Be good to Miss Thing."

"Buster, Angel Doll," Kitty cooed as he walked her graciously to our door.

've never let a man go down on me before, but I will let you do it, K-K, if you tell me truthfully something I have always wanted to know about queers," the nasal-sounding radiologist friend of mine said one late evening to Kitty.

"What's that, buddy?" K-K asked, sitting in the doctor's Sears, Roebuck version of a Danish chair, sipping a double Scotch and soda.

"When does a queer know he's a queer?" the doctor asked, sitting across from K-K, sipping a gin and tonic.

"I don't know about all homo-sex-u-als," K-K said, crossing his legs and pointing his Gucci loafers' toes toward the floor. "I only know about me. I didn't know that I was queer, as you so graciously put it, until I was in junior high. I overheard the gym teacher tell his locker room clerk to watch that queer Kurt. 'Assign him a locker close to your desk,' he ordered. I guess he identified me when he caught me sitting down pissing or something. I never do use those God-awful stinky urinals unless I'm looking for some quick trade.

"I have known that I was homosexual since the time I was about thirteen. My brother John was sick, couldn't collect his newspapers one Saturday. So I collected for him. At this one apartment building, this—I guess you would call him a fairy—answered the door," K-K said, wrapping a cocktail napkin around his icy glass. "He was wearing a loose gown and reeked of perfume, had on a few dabs of rouge and a lot of diamond rings on his very manicured hands. He was drinking out of a silver goblet. One look at me and he forgot all about sodomy laws. I was prettier than I am now, if you can imagine that could be possible," Kitty stated. He was dressed in a white polished cotton suit, a Brooks Brothers blue striped shirt, and a paisley tie. He was very tan from a winter in Jamaica. His long black hair was carefully styled to show off his widow's peak and flowed like a lion's mane nearly to his shoulders.

"I had a head of dark curly hair then and the face of an angel. This old faggot, as you could call him," he said, smiling at my friend Tooloose, "asked me to please come inside while he got some change for me. A Bach organ duet was playing in the background somewhere. His apartment was not to be believed, all silk brocade, crystal chandeliers, fresh flowers," K-K said, lost in the memory of his initiation. "I could smell turkey and sausage stuffing cooking in his kitchen, hear pans clattering.

"'I'm having a birthday party for a friend tonight,' he said, switching out his bedroom with my money. 'Would you like to come? There will be some other young men here your age. I'd like you to be my special guest,' he said, squeezing a five-dollar bill into my hand. 'Keep the change for taxi fare tonight. I'll expect you at eight o'clock,' he said, giving me a Marlene Dietrich smile as he ushered me out the door.

"That night, babies, I told Mama and Daddy that I was tired from collecting for John and went to bed early. I locked my room door, got dressed in the suit I wore to mass, and climbed out the window. I almost ran all the way.

"I found out later that my host was a Presbyterian minister, doctorate of divinity. He answered the door dressed in a long black silk robe, smelled better than earlier. 'Come, come,' he beckoned, 'meet my friends!' I could hear Judy Garland singing 'Somewhere Over the Rainbow.' I knew it was Judy because at thirteen I was an old-movie buff," K-K said, accepting a fresh drink from Tooloose. "My father used to really get mad when I would stay inside on weekends and holidays looking at old movies instead of playing Cowboys and Indians with the other boys. I didn't like their kind of ballplaying, either. I've watched *Camille* thirty-three times," said K-K, sipping his drink.

"The lights were dimmed in the living room. As my eyes adjusted to the change, I saw a room filled with men, older men and boys, all beautifully dressed, sipping out of silver goblets and nibbling on hors d'oeuvres. My host took me by the hand and walked me over to a table loaded with champagne bottles on ice, silver goblets, and silver trays of hors d'oeuvres. He asked me my name.

"'It's Kurt,' I responded very demurely. 'Kurt? I'll call you Kitty-Kat. That's what you look like, a pretty little fluffy kitty kat.'

"Babies," he said, "I had the time of my life. I still see him occasionally. We still party."

"That's how you found out?" Tooloose asked.

"Exactly! Now remember, you promised," K-K said, smiling as he got up and walked over to my friend's chair.

"I changed my mind," Tooloose stated, rising and grabbing my hand, coyly squeezing it. "I don't want to find out. Suppose I find out that I like it, too?" he asked, smiling back at Kitty.

C ome on, Toots, fuck me," Kitty said from his side of our bed. He wasn't smiling as he lay there looking across the studio room at me sitting on the toilet in our tiny bathroom. Kitty referred to it as our poolroom sometimes. "Let's make a baby. Me and you, Lewis. We can do it. I love you," he said when I reentered the room. How tempting he looked, too, lying there with his long, wavy dark brown hair spread across his pillow. Don't hurt him, Lewis, I thought as I approached that bed. Maybe his eyes told me not to hurt him. "We could make a baby. You want one. I want one, too. I'd be the best daddy in all of the world. Lots of my gayest friends are such good daddies. Lewis, we could even get married. I think I'd like to marry you," he said as I bent down to get on the bed. "You could lock me up on Fridays in the nursery or something. Maybe I could kick my Jones if I had a baby," he said as I sat across his knees going slowly down on his friend.

Baby, I am tired of silly-willies like Woo-dy boy thinking that I want their old bodies," Kitty murmured. He was wrapping his soft, satiny body around my naked back and looking at Woody, talking to Woody. Woody was squeezing my hands under the cover.

"Last night Woo-dy was really enjoying me on his little short wee-wee. He was oh-ing, ah-ing, stroking my hair until he opened his eyes and saw it was Kit-ty. That's when I got my usual pat on the head and the 'Now, Kitty.'" Kitty leaned over my shoulder, grimacing at a cherub-looking Woody. Woody was squeezing my hand. "Buster, I am the pretty, sexy one. You are the potbellied eunuch. You, Miss Woo-dy, should be flattered that I make overtures to you. Why should I want you? You ain't got nothing but a technician's title. Dr. Woody, allergist," Kitty said, running his hands through my curly hair.

"Except the money, Lewis, and this bed that I am about to put your pretty sexy ass out of unless you shut up and go to sleep," Woody said. His eyes were closed, nose turned up.

"Bully boy, you just try to put me out of here," K-K said, mocking a small stubborn boy. "Me and Lewis will team up and kick your flat flabby behind. Nowadays, you know, us girls are closing our ranks. No longer will you brawny brutes use y'all's muscles to subdue us," Kitty said, widening his beautiful Doberman eyes. He was rubbing my nipples as he called me to his arms. "Unite with me, Lewis," he commanded. "What have you got to lose but your chains?"

"My ex-husband, his checks, my status, free rent," I drowsily said.

"Freedom," Woody added. "Freedom to travel, to dissipate, to sleep late, to leave bills behind."

"Freedom to fly excellent but unemployed fashion illustrators like you from New York to Detroit for orgies," I said, releasing my nipples from K-K's fingertips. I was cuddling up to Woody's paunchy stomach now.

SAGE

You've seen those Masai Africans on television travel shows. They're the really tall ones that wear bright red blanket-like robes draped over their slender, muscled bodies. If they came in yellow skin, Sage, dressed like that, would have looked like one of them. He would have preferred looking more like Lauren Hutton, however. Clothed in his favorite jeans, boots, and a silk shirt, he only weighed a hundred and sixty-one pounds without the forty pounds of gold he always wore. He told me that he was beautifully striking in an ugly sort of way. No hair decorated his razor-marked skin. All Sage got when he tried to grow a beard and a mustache were little beady red balls, and never quite enough of them. A receding hairline was disguised by keeping his hair closely clipped. This hairstyle enhanced his forehead, making it appear even more protruding. A high forehead sometimes gives a person an appearance of being an outer space creature. Perched above a nose that had an almost visible bridge, this forehead made Sage look extremely intelligent; he was, too. His nose flared when he was angry, though he was rarely angry with anyone but me. High cheekbones were set above small, perfect lips that covered a mouthful of tiny teeth that Sage had spent Cadillac money on repairing. A Modigliani neck connected his head to shoulders and arms that were those of a dancer. His arms were all muscle and skin, no flab. They were covered with fine golden-red hair. His hands were big and ringless. This one knew what not to emphasize. A huge collection of fine belts were used to accent his twenty-eight-inch waist. And his hips were perfect for bikinis, as they melted into his thighs without any disruption of fat. His thighs and his long legs were also covered with fine golden-reddish hairs. I liked his laughter best of all. It sounded like applause.

This particular evening he was gliding around our kitchen, preparing a late supper for himself. Ciarra, our Vietnamese roommate, only ate lunch. I was dieting. Living with *Vogue*-like roommates can keep you dieting. Only later did I learn that they cheated by using cocaine and amphetamines as appetite depressants. See, I had them robbed of their earthly belongings after they forced me out of our apartment. I should say *my* apartment, since I'm the one that found it. Hidden in with Sage's collection of freak pictures I found enough amphetamines to last for a year. In Ciarra's paintbrush set I found a bottle that contained about five grams of cocaine still in the rocks.

The African robe he wore as he moved from stove to refrigerator to counter was powder blue. White hand embroidery trimmed its V-neck and its billowy sleeves. Robes were his favorite clothing. He'd gotten used to them in the days when he had been an Episcopalian priest. Sage left the church for the same reason he had left teaching at an eastern Ivy League university. He got bored. He was presently secretary-companion to an alcoholic New York aristocrat whose granddaddies had made more money than he could ever use. The trust wouldn't let him give it away, even if he had ever contemplated such an act. The church, that Ivy League school, and "Thee," as we called his boss, had gotten Sage accustomed to the best.

Our kitchen was a working kitchen. James Beard and Julia Child both would have approved. Ciarra had printed on our wall in Vietnamese one of Sage's favorite sayings in black letters: "Let's all try to act like ladies." We told inquisitive outsiders that it said whatever we thought was interesting at the moment. "A stitch in time saves nine" or "God bless the child who's got his own" or "Fuck off."

"Ciarra said that I can watch if you agree," he said in that slow, clipped method he had adopted.

"Watch what?"

"Watch you two ball her new friend, Guy."

"Gimme a piece of fried chicken and we'll ball you. And you can watch us ball each other, too."

"Wait until I smother it in the gravy."

"Nope, can't wait and can't eat the butter sauce anyway. I'm dieting," I said.

"Chile, you aren't ever going to make a lady. You're too impatient," he said, preparing his tray.

"Maybe not," I commented, really getting into that breast, "but you aren't going to ever make one either, fella, no matter how patient you are."

Ignoring my smart remark, he completed setting his tray of chicken, steamed buttered carrots, and asparagus with his special hollandaise sauce by carefully placing a white starched napkin on it.

"Ready?"

"Ready!" I responded. "Follow me, man. Showtime on Fifth Avenue, get your seats right here," I called out, carny style. "I've got the perfect seat for you, honey," I said, looking back at Sage following me through our living room.

My room was right next to his, only half the size of his. Mine was prettier, however. He had hung plants in ceramic pots by long leather straps from my twelve-foot beams. The city's lights filtered through my sky-light twenty-four hours a day. Waking up in that room was like waking up in a botanical garden. That lighting, mixed with my rheostat control, made the room tranquil all of the time. Near the door a walnut Parsons table held a clear crystal vase of pink carnations and baby's breath and an eighteenth-century leather Bible. Anything to prevent me from cluttering that lovely wooden table with cosmetics and perfume bottles. Woody had sent me the flowers.

Centered in the middle of my room was my huge bed. It was covered in a gray down-filled coverlet, gray sheets, and lots of pillows whose cases were all monogrammed *L* in red, just like my sheets. Mounted in the middle of my cushions were Ciarra and Guy, high on opium. My room smelled like a field of lavender-scented flowers.

Sage stopped and slipped out of his slides on the Oriental runner that ran down our walnut-stained hallway floor. My floor was covered in gray carpeting. You know, the kind so thick you have to have the bottom of your doors shaved so that they can close over it.

I said nothing to them. Sage didn't either. He was following my lead. Reaching my closet, I stopped and slid open the door. I then signaled to Sage to sit on top of this eight-foot cedar ladder I kept there to help me water the plants. Handing me his tray, Sage hiked up his robe like a lady about to ascend a winding staircase. Seated on top, he smiled down diva-style at me and reached for his dinner.

"Not until I get a real kiss," I said, withholding his tray. He bent down. I tippy-toed up to his lips. Caressing in this way, I whispered, "Bon appétit, baby." Then I handed him his tray. Turning around slowly, I took off my silk tartan plaid robe and let it slink down my body. This was before I had to suck in my stomach to look good naked.

I slowly walked to my bed and them, wondering what I was to do next. Ciarra was the director tonight.

"Lewis, have a little smoke with me and my friend Guy. It's so good," she said as she pulled back the covers for me. "Guy," she directed lazily, "reach down on the floor and give me my box."

Her box was an antique straw hatbox that Sage had found in Thee's storage room at one or another of his homes. It was faded blue and yellow. Thee's hatbox became Ciarra's dream box. It held a potpourri of drugs and related paraphernalia. Thai sticks, hashish, Percodan, blue Valiums, Quaaludes, Dexedrine, cocaine in the rock, and the black glass she needed.

Ciarra looked like an Oriental doll. Vietnamese doll, she would say. The only thing that could really disturb her was for someone to think she was Japanese. She hated the Japanese.

"The best for the best," she hissed out. She always sounded like she was giving orders when she spoke English. Calmly, carefully, she pulled the opium to the top of the heap. Unwrapping the tinfoil that covered it, she shaved off a few tiny pieces. Then she lifted out a small aluminum-covered tray and handed it to Guy. Finding her ebony lighter, she lit the opium, cooked it until it began to smoke, then passed it to me.

"Hurry. Don't lose it. Join us," she invited, slowly descending back into my pillows.

As I inhaled that thick, lavender-smelling smoke, I concentrated on our audience. A thirty-four-year-old man never touched by a woman is up there watching, I mused. Maybe he'll join us this time. Ciarra had tried to seduce him once. I had never tried. Reaching down to the floor, I placed her little foil-covered tray on my carpeting. Wonder if we look as unreal to him as he looks to me, I thought.

"Suppose we could make him choose between eating and watching?" I whispered to them.

"Let's let him eat first. That way we'll never have to know what he preferred, us or it. It would be humiliating to have him crunching in the midst of our thing," Ciarra whispered back.

"Could cause me some technical problems," Guy quietly added.

Sage thrust the covers off us the moment he climbed off the ladder to place his empty tray on the floor. As he scrambled back up that ladder, he looked just like a late theatergoer. You've seen 'em trying to get to their seat after the curtain has risen. Ciarra began by parting her legs slightly. Then she began touching herself slowly, staring at Sage the entire time. She stroked herself; we all watched. Sage watched us. We watched him. His mouth was cracked open just the slightest. He held his hands crisscrossed up to his chest. Sage wasn't going to chance touching his It. He was too ladylike for exhibitionism.

"One thing I know for sure I am," Ciarra said, purring, "I'm s-e-x-y. I am very sexy." She was massaging her opening, pulling her pubic hairs, sliding her finger in and out, up and down.

Guy was trying hard not to ad-lib. I spread and began to follow her lead. Then Guy followed me. I watched Sage, we all watched Sage. I felt weightless and rather sensual myself for a change. Exhibitions generally bored me. Ciarra turned and began to kiss Guy. He in turn began to kiss me. Then we were all kissing each other from the neck up. Her thick hair felt heavy. She began to moan as she kissed me now. Guy was lost in her small olive thighs. I could tell by his slurping sounds and her rigid tongue on me that she was coming. Resting only long enough to slide down to me, she led us into the next scene, her back door and my front. I laid back and watched the other three. Occasionally, I would stroke myself. She "ummmed" loudly. I remained silent. I always remained silent at these shows.

When I awakened, my bedroom contained only the smell of opium and sunlight. I could hear koto music coming from Sage's room.

Getting up, picking up my robe, I went over to Ciarra's room. Ciarra lay in a corner on a straw mat, buttoned up in a yellow, down-filled comforter. Ciarra was a painter. Her room was her studio. Shelves of painter's equipment lined her walls; a drop cloth covered her wooden floor. Right beneath her skylight she had placed her easel. The piece on the easel at the time was beginning to look like an orchid. You could tell by the center of the flower where she had begun.

"It's what some wear, some use, some abuse, some want," she had said, trying to make a riddle when I wanted her to confirm what I saw. "It's a . . ." Here I feigned a blush.

"That's correct," she said, winking at me.

Slipping down onto her mat, I kissed her on the nape

of the neck. "Miss Saigon, do you know what? You are sexy. Where's your friend?"

"Don't you hear the music? He's with the music," she said softly, molding her behind into my stomach. "You and me? We fell asleep. They didn't," she said, licking me in long laps on the side of my face.

PRINCE

Kitty brought Prince into my life. He'd recruited him for one of our orgyettes. As he and Raoul, one of his new pets, cruised Woodward, Raoul spotted Prince trying to interest someone in buying a watch. Raoul invited him back to my house for the set before Kitty could stop him, so Kitty said. Seems like Raoul and Prince had met at Jackson Prison. Prince brewed the finest spud juice in the joint, Raoul had proudly acknowledged. And at one time, Raoul said, Prince had led a gang of two thousand in Detroit. They called him the Quaker Prince back then.

All I noticed about him at first was that he needed a pair of shoes; he was wearing slightly run-over white Swedish clogs on a cold day in late autumn. What I noticed after that was that he was not participating in our activities. He simply sat quietly, chain-smoking some quite exquisite herb and tooting up our white lady.

I didn't pay any serious attention to him until I became conscious of this lighter clicking on and off somewhere in the room during the midst of the orgyette. Peeping between Kitty's legs as he changed positions, I located the source of the click—Prince. He was sitting fully clothed on the couch, flicking his lighter periodically to illuminate the scene on the floor.

Later he told me that if it hadn't been for the cocaine Kitty had stuffed his nose with on the way over, he'd have fallen asleep on us. I went to sleep myself, watching him watch us. When I awakened, I was in my bed. He was sprawled there beside me, smoking a joint, dressed in a pair of Woody's pajamas. I peeped at him, trying to decide if he was the rapist. He certainly looked the part: small recessed eyes, thick nose, pouting mouth, moist lips, strong hands.

Then I remembered how the party had ended. Kitty had slithered over to him and tried to unzip his pants. Then I heard some soft talking. Then Kitty had slithered back to me. I'd closed my eyes to pretend I was asleep so that Kitty wouldn't become embarrassed by another rejection. And I had gone to sleep for real.

"What did you whisper to Kitty-Kat?" I opened with

this. No "Hello," no "What are you doing in my bedroom?," no "Why are you wearing my ex-husband's pajamas?" "What did you say to my friend?" I repeated.

"I told him, 'Never in the free world.' I told him that I was prepared to see to it he lost an organ if he didn't scat. I told him that the only punk in that crowd that I wanted to have touch me was the pretty yellow girl."

"So, where'd you find the silk pajamas?" I asked, rising.

"Your friend Woody came over here as I was putting you to bed. He said he lived on the other side of your apartment. We got to talking over a beer and I told him I'd just come back from Frisco. Didn't have a place yet. He suggested that I stay here on his side until he got back from this sailboat race on the East Coast. He gave me these to wear. Didn't think you'd mind the company. Told me the two of you used to be married until you tired of being an adulteress."

After Prince left, Woody swore that he missed him more than I did. "Took the weight off us, didn't he?" Keep Prince happy and he was the perfect housewife. I couldn't out-cook him, out-iron him, or out-fuck him. No one could. Unhappy, he could turn into a B-rated monster. One time he emptied a grill of steaks and hot coals off our balcony as I walked past. He thought I was going out to cheat on him and Woody.

The last evening he spent with us was a memorable one. It was one of those football Sundays in January. I imagine I was the only one in the world not watching. Woody and his lady, Cookie, were at the game. I was lying in bed waiting on my Valiums to balance the Bloody

Marys I'd consumed for brunch, listening to live gospel music over WGPR. At some point I decided that a cold bottle of champagne would probably do the trick, chase the devils away with one of their own kind. So up I got and sallied into the kitchen. Prince was loudly singing "Precious Lord," standing in front of the oven while he basted two capons. Homemade Parker House rolls were rising on the counter. Happy? He was radiant, had on this floor-length silk caftan that he'd had made out of some leftover fabric from Woody's bathroom drapes and shower curtains. Print tigers and leopards and elephants grazing through a jungle. An ashtray on the counter let me know that he was exactly where he wished to be— high, high, high. Woody kept Prince the very best weed "for security purposes."

"Wait until y'all taste this cornbread dressing," he said, pushing the tray back into the oven. "Woody's gonna dig these turnips and mustards, too." He cut the heat off from beneath a steaming pot. "See, I don't overcook my greens the way some people do," he said, feeling my ass as I took the champagne out of the refrigerator. "Woody likes them crunchy."

I didn't feel a bit of jealousy. I was walking out of the kitchen when he called out to me.

"Hey, girl! Don't you think this is cute?"

I turned to find Prince with his back to me, bent over in the process of lifting his robe over his head. Before I could close my eyes there he was, looking at me from between his bare legs.

"Cute, ain't it?" he asked.

"Beautiful," I said. I tried not to frown the way I would have had he not been staring at me. I hated the sight of naked men. For some reason I smiled and slowly started walking toward him with that cold bottle of champagne in my hand. I remember reading the year on the label, quickly unpeeling the foil and unhooking the wires. He must have suspected what I was going to do but he didn't move, just waited patiently. The sound that bottle made when I withdrew the cork sounded like all of the New Year's Eve *pop*s I've ever heard combined. Before I lost one bubble, I had that bottle aimed at his ass. "Happy New Year, Prince," I heard myself say as it trickled down his butt, through his crease. He didn't say a word, just waited. Slowly I inserted the neck of that bottle. His squeal sounded like two hundred pigs.

"Go on!" he ordered. "That's it, ba-bee. Force it out of me." It ran free onto the floor, thick like Brie on the run. He remained bent over while I lovingly extracted the neck of that bottle. Then he dropped to his knees and started laughing. "I'm all yours now. You mine?" he asked, stroking himself.

"Sometimes," I said, looking at his backside and wishing he'd pull his gown down.

P rince is dead, baby," he announced on the telephone. "I killed him last night. He tried to fuck with my mind. I'm gonna miss the fella. We've been together since I was a kid. I buried him this morning in his club jacket. You know, the one he and I embroidered his name on the back of when we were fifteen. I placed an ounce of excellent grass in his jacket pocket."

"Where'd you bury him?" I asked, peering out of my hotel window at the phone booth across the street. I thought he might have been calling from that booth. It was empty.

"I buried him in a pile of garbage in back of the county jail. He wouldn't have been comfortable anywhere else. Take me back!"

"No!"

"I'm sorry about what happened. That was Prince that threatened your date, baby. Prince is old-fashioned. He never understood that his woman was free to see other men. He was pre-revolutionary."

"Prince didn't have a woman. Neither did you, Joseph Conrad Jones. My man pays in cash. You were my paid companion, not my man. His name is Woody."

"I was paid by Woody? Then I'm like an employee of his, huh?"

"Right," I said.

"Then actually you don't have the authority to fire me. Do you? I should be begging Woody to give me back my job, not you. Right?"

"Right!" I said, remembering his work.

"Come on, Lewis. Come on out and play with me. I miss you."

"You miss Woody's checks."

"Then I miss y'all. I need a little fun. I'm tired, Lewis, I've been sleeping on people's couches. I've lost you because of him and him because of you. That leaves me with nobody but me. You know how confused I get out here by myself. Prince was at home in the street. I am not. I need my job back."

Loneliness, maybe, a sense of fair play, thoughts of his lovings—something made me promise to meet him.

"I'll meet you in an hour on the Boulevard and Second. If Prince isn't dead, Joseph, I'm going to kill him myself. Our problem is that I don't know how to separate his behavior from your body."

He came loping down the Boulevard with his hands in his jean pockets. Rancid sweat began to leak out of my body. I hoped my scent would reach him before I did. For a moment he stopped and looked into Milgrim's old window. I thought he was gonna turn around until I saw he was pissing. I started to drive off. Maybe he hasn't seen me yet. Avoid him, Lewis. He's crazy, really crazy. All that talk about killing Prince. He *is* Prince. Without Prince, he's only another broken fantasy. Run, Lewis, I commanded myself.

"You can't run, Lewis." Sestra was talking now. "Once you run, Lewis, your eyes will lose the madness. The madness protects you. The smell will go away. It protects you. Girl, it took a long time for this protection system to be developed. I almost lost it. I wanted to be an ordinary woman. In fact, I wanted to be a lady. Know what happened? Guess! I was attacked by a complete stranger. He would have killed me had the madness not returned as he beat me, as he tried to rape me. Know what I did? I asked him to please let me taste it. The moment he was about to come, I bit him hard enough for him to let go of me. Before he could move I butted him in the chin with my head. Then my nails dug into his balls. I knocked him out momentarily that way. Then I jumped out of my car and ran screaming into Jefferson. Madness thought up the plan. Sanity would have made me submit. Don't break the cord," she ordered.

Five days on the street, I thought, he reverts to a convict. Look at that walk. He walks as if he were chained!

As he continued to move toward my car, my breathing became heavy. My tongue felt thick. I remembered I had seen a man kick a woman in the street once. Everybody just watched except for an old woman carrying a plain brown paper shopping bag on her arm. That old woman reached down into her bag and pulled out an ice pick. "Kick her again, son, and you got to deal with me and this," she said, showing him the ice pick. "I killed a man with an ax that beat me—killed him while he was awake." She was steadily walking toward him. The woman he had attacked ran as he stood paralyzed by the old woman's intervention. Men don't expect that from women. When she got near him, he yelled out:

"I quit! I don't wanna fight you, Granny."

"Why not? Scared I might let loose on you?"

There was no little old lady on the Boulevard that night. No one but the two of us.

"Hi, baby," he said, walking up to the car and getting in. "I missed you, baby."

"You missed an easy mark. I brought you some smoke and enough money to check into a hotel," I said, really looking at him for the first time. I wanted to feel him inside me again. Hear us laugh.

"You miss Prince, ba-bee? All that farting and fucking he did?"

I grinned in confession as I started up the car.

ROBB

obb was tickling my nose with an ostrich feather. I was fighting to awaken, lying naked in his loft bed. "Pretty lady, pretty lady, it's time to wake up," the King of Swing was saying to me. "Your old man is ready to go now. Roberta has worn him out. As for you, you slept through some scenes that might even have gotten you off. You have the honor of being the first chick to ever go to sleep while I was doing her. Roberta was amazed. She slipped away from Woody, where she was really working to test you out. You purred only. Please don't let this experience filter around Manhattan. We'd be laughed off the best sets. Come on, Lewis," Robb cooed at me. "Wake up."

"I'm awake," I said. We were lying perched closer to

his ceiling than to his floor. His specially designed loft bed was ten feet off the ground. You reached it by this ladder. In one corner at the foot there was a small refrigerator containing Godiva chocolates, small bottles of fine champagne, rocks of cocaine, marijuana, and amyl nitrates. You ate the candy out of the box, drank the champagne out of the bottles, blew the coke off your fingertips, and smoked all you wanted. In the corner was a small color television used only for basketball games. At the head of the bed was a control switch for operating a stereo downstairs in Robb's living room. Only rules, you couldn't smoke cigarettes, drink hard liquor, dance standing up, or wear clothes. We called these "Robb's Rules of Order."

"Why are you torturing me with that feather?" I asked, opening my eyes and looking up at him.

"I'm trying to get you up," he whispered in a faint Brooklyn accent. "Woody wants to go for breakfast. I think," he whispered, "Rebecca and Bee have sapped him out. Thought you said he was dull, baby doll. They thought he was great. 'Course, good sex to you is unused. Your mama tell you that? Or are you an old closet masturbator?"

"I never masturbate," I lied, looking off at the refrigerator.

"Never? That's why you're sick! No one should be able

to love you better than you can love yourself, doll. That is real independence." With this, he pulled back the pink sheets that covered me and spread my legs.

"I just want to make sure you've got a working one. Every time I've felt it it has been moistened with that grape jelly. Let's see if it's self-starting," he said, beginning to tap my little lady with his index finger. "Do you feel that? You do? Then it's connected."

He looked so professional, so serious, peering and tapping, that I laughed. "That's a girl. Sex should be fun." Before long I was as involved as he. He was spanking her, squeezing her with his fingertips, caressing her.

"Man, you have got a real one. And she's pretty, too."

It's going to work, I thought to myself, watching him love me. I feel it! I cried inside. "I feel it!" I heard myself scream.

"Shh," he said, resting his head on my stomach. "Congratulations, Lewis," he whispered. "It works. It truly works."

FLOWER

think we could say that I was feeling maudlin that early summer night. Six extra-dry vodka martinis with dilled Brussels sprouts and dinner alone in Detroit can make a monk feel maudlin. I was also tired of Little Harry's cocktail pianist. That pianist was for sure not Bobby Short. He reminded me a bit of my piano teacher, Mr. Alpino. My mother had insisted that I learn to play piano. She had always wanted to learn, it seemed. Mr. Alpino, I guess, needed the two dollars per hour. He certainly did not need my banging out the three Bs.

Little Harry's was full of bunches of middle-aged affluent blond people on their way out of Detroit before it really got dark. Every now and then one drunken account executive or another would burst out in song; you know the type I mean. And that silky, shrunken pianist would bang out the melody.

I slid out of my red leather seat, stumbling only a little, and tipped over to the piano.

"Say, Charlie, how about playing 'Meditations,'" I asked loudly. "If we're going to make this joint an old church, let's play a hymn I wanna hear."

All the people at the piano bar grinned nervously. The one Black man that was there didn't. He just looked on blankly. Guess he was comparing my aggressiveness with the quietness of his little polyester-draped blond date.

"Sure, Lewis," the pianist said as he graciously accepted the five-dollar bill I laid on his tray.

If he played "Meditations," either I didn't recognize it or I didn't hear it. Angered by what I presumed was a slight instead of a lack of talent, I blurted out:

"Y'all are in Motown, you know, not Germany, nor Italy, nor Grosse Pointe. Charlie, how about Ray Charles or Stevie Wonder?" I asked.

"How about 'Just the Way You Are'?" a soft lady's voice asked from a corner of that tired old room.

"Don't know it," Charlie responded.

"I do," she said one note above a whisper. That's when I saw her. She was wearing a man-tailored double-breasted black silk suit with a hot pink silk blouse. She was so fair and her hair so ashy. The most amazing thing about her was her size. She must have weighed three hundred and seventy-five pounds naked. Yet her face was not fat, just rounded and very beautiful.

As she approached Charlie's bench, the room became quiet. The young bartender even stopped shaking a cocktail he was making. She walked like a dancer, erect, slowly and assuredly. Graciously, she slid a bill on Charlie's tray, sat down, and began to play and sing.

"Don't go changing . . . Just the way you are."

The Black man sitting at the piano bar began to hum, then whistle, then sing behind her. They stopped in the same way that they began—elegantly. Outside of their music, they never touched each other. I don't think they even looked at each other.

"My name is Little Flower," she said. "People that like me call me Flower," she said, sitting down across from me. I could see that she was a real redhead, freckles and all. Her gold-framed, rose-tinted glasses made her blue eyes look gray. She sat on the edge of a too-small chair, lighting up the first of an endless series of Turkish-smelling cigarettes. The tiny ebony gold-trimmed holder that she held between long unpainted manicured nails was rich. She looked rich, too. That is, if you overlooked her peacock's suit and concentrated on her. Her teeth had been pampered all of her life. The fair skin unblemished, almost translucent. Her fat even looked lush. I imagined her walking the streets of Florence in a long black flowing cape. Her perfume was thick. There is something about the way perfumes mix with obese flesh that makes you want to get closer.

"My name is Lewis. Thanks for the ditty. It was needed. You a musician?"

"No, I'm a collector. I collect pretty broken things and make them prettier. I sell some of them for a living. How about some seltzer water and a wedge of lime? I drink it all of the time. It's good for you."

"Sounds good to me, Flower. Only, have the bartender add a couple of shots of vodka with mine. I'm not that concerned about what's good for me. I like what *feels* good to me."

"You won't accept seltzer and lime without vodka, huh? That's too bad, Lewis."

"Why's that, Flower?"

"'Cause that means you'll have to buy your own drink. I don't buy pretty things drinks. It breaks them." She was peering over her tinted glasses now, still sitting on the edge of that too-little chair.

"And that means I'll drink alone, then. The way I was doing. Thanks for the song. Do you need a waiter to help lift you off the edge of that chair or can you lift yourself, Miss Healthy?" I was giving her my crazy Lewis stare without stopping. "Those foreign cigarettes stink, too."

"Tough," she said. "You're really tough. It would have been fun," she said, lifting herself daintily from that too-small seat.

Watching her walk away from me like a giant bull elephant grazing through a jungle, I felt maudlin again. I felt like sleeping, sleeping.

George, Little Harry's parking attendant, was waiting on me at the bottom of those green outdoor-carpeted steps. Occasionally, George walked me across the street home if I got wrecked after lunch. He reminded me of all of my uncles. George was probably earning more money in tips than Big Harry. I adored his style. "There's a lady waiting on you, Miss Lewis," he said. "She asked me to ask you to come over to her car when you came out." George was at least six foot five and one-half inches, Hershey bar brown.

"Did she pay you, too?" I asked with only a slight slur.

"A twenty," he said. "You gonna do it?"

"For you, for sure, George," I said as he walked up those steep steps to help me down them.

"Her car is the pink Caddy over there. She's a real lady. Her father is a big preacher in town."

"*Now that we've found love, what are we gonna do?*" blasted out of her car tape deck as George opened the door for me to get in. She looked lush, stuffed into the driver's half of the front seat, and she smelled like lavender. Her skin was even fairer than it had appeared in the darkened restaurant. Three tastefully selected rings decorated her long, slender fingers. One ring was a cluster of diamonds that formed a butterfly with emerald eyes. The second ring was pink gold with a square-cut amethyst. The third ring was a wide, plain gold wedding band worn on her right baby finger.

Later that night, after she found love in me, she told me about herself. Her former husband was an international Middle Eastern dealer of antiques. They had divorced three years ago, their two boys going to him. He couldn't see his boys growing up in a dyke's household. That was his favorite name for her, she said. We were sprawling in her brass bed when she told me this.

"You think of yourself as a stud?" I asked. "A dyke? My friends and I simply think of ourselves as free. 'Dyke' sounds as ancient as 'fairy,'" I said to her as she began to make love to me again. "Dyke, pronounced *Dykay*, was a Greek goddess of love, you know," I said to her as she nuzzled her head between my thighs. She was quick and smooth. "You ever hear of Sappho? Now, she was really something . . . That feels good," I said as she rocked my boat. "You feel good," I said, stretching out and letting her love me.

And she smelled so good. Her thick red hair felt like dolls' hair as she rubbed herself on my knee, gently. I felt her dampness. It was warm as it flowed. I felt myself open up to her, reach out to her. I wished that I could love a woman as Flower loved me.

After she had satisfied herself and me, she held me and we cried. She tried to entice me when she sensed I was ready to leave her.

"Hungry? I have some great king crab legs just waiting."

"Nope."

"Want some different music? I guess the Third World is tired of finding love."

"I love 'em. Leave 'em on," I said, sitting up. "Who's she?" I was looking at a photograph of a little brown woman lying naked on the beach.

"That's Blake," she said, lighting up one of those heavy Turkish cigars. "We were married once—in church—by a liberal minister. I wore a tuxedo and everything. I used to dress in drag a lot. The wedding ring I wear was hers. One day she threw it at me. Pronounced me a bawdy, bizarre bitch. Said our marriage was a joke. Before I knew it, I had knocked her out with a right hook I didn't even know I had. When she came to, I had cut off her hair, slashed up her clothes that I bought, and had Bo-Bo pick her up. Bo-Bo's my boys' bodyguard-housekeeper. She calls me every now and then, says she's real sorry."

"I bet she is," I said, looking around her bedroom for the first time. It was filled with good taste and wealth.

"Wanna go someplace?" she asked, embracing me. She was ready to go at it again.

"Yep, I do," I said, giving her a peck on her satiny cheek. "Home. I wanna go home," I said, sitting up in that bed, staring at Blake's picture.

AUGUS

I didn't scream when I awakened and noted a foreign pair of hands were clinging to me, long hands. Their manicured nails almost touched my nipples. I knew from past experience that they belonged to a guest of Kitty's. Kitty was backed up against me, feigning sleep. I knew he was pretending because he never, never slept while one of his guests visited. Usually he locked them inside our apartment, too. Sestra had to wisely point out that she felt it was awfully daring of me to allow this. "Fool, just what do you think you are gonna do in case one of your little darling 'guests' responds negatively to y'all's little games?" I didn't bother to tell her that Kitty had drilled me on what to do. I was to throw this bottle of pure lye on the insurrector, then run into the bathroom, bolt the door, and plug in the telephone we kept hidden in the clothes hamper. Kitty in the meanwhile would run out into the garden and scream for help. The "guest," now scared and scarred, would be met by the NYPD just as he managed to unbolt the door.

"He asleep?" the guest asked in a slight West Indian accent. "He oughta be. Your brother, man, has an unquenchable appetite. Our hostess threw him off our set." Kitty, it seems, had staged one of his drunk-and-disorderly scenes. The Japanese hostess had been on the verge of serving homemade red bean ice cream and coconut macaroons when Kitty waltzed out of her powder room wearing only some of her perfume and offered himself as dessert. What could be more perfect after an exquisite dinner than lovemaking? Kitty reasoned. The stranger's fingertips were perched on my breasts by the time he got to this.

"What could be?" I responded.

"I agreed!" The guest was now stroking my nipples.

"He is a brazen bitch. But an honest one," I said. The stranger was trying to press himself into my crease. I tightened up, refusing him.

"Release me," I demanded in a normal voice.

"Why?" he asked in a whisper. He really didn't want to waken Kitty.

"I wanna see you," I responded, turning. "I like your hands," I said as he let go. "What's your name?"

"Augus," he said, kissing my nose. He looked like a young tanned Paul Newman. "What would you like for breakfast, pretty lady?"

"Kitty and you," Kitty blurted out, flipping over into my back, facing Augus.

like the posture Augus takes," Sestra said in my inner ear as I leaped out of a Checker cab onto Seventh Avenue. "What's that?" I asked, hopping over some drunk's breakfast. "The one that's most appropriate, dummy," she whispered. I heard the Greek church music as I bounded up the stairs leading to his loft. Some immigrant Greek sect held church on the floor beneath Augus's.

He peeped out of the hole in the door, letting out a "Shit, man" as he unbolted it and opened. I was steaming. Sweat trickled down the crack in my ass from my shoulders. "Slow down, sister," Sestra suggested.

"What do you want, Lewis?"

"Your ass, Augus!"

"That's different. Really different. What happened? You mix your venom with some Spanish fly?" His voice remained soft as I shoved him aside. "Slow down, man!" he ordered. "It's God's day of rest."

His loft smelled like old earwax and spit mixed. Reefer roaches curled up on the floor with cigarette butts and gum wrappers. Plastic cups sprawled in corners and on cigarette-burned cocktail tables, traces of red wine splattered on their sides. Augus usually cleaned up after his disco parties at dawn on Monday. That way he could scoop up his debris, wrap it in green garbage bags, and sneak it in among his neighbors' identically wrapped trash. Augus lived in New York's garment district, where the city didn't provide daily service. The businessmen in the area had to pay a fee for the disposal. Augus rode his neighbors piggyback in his efforts to pull himself up by his bootstraps.

As he rebolted the heavy steel door, my eyes adjusted to the candlelight. Electricity was consumed only during business hours since he'd lost a seventeen-hundred-dollar battle with the power company. Two years before, a small film company had rented his "studio." He, it seems, out of ignorance and desperation for their fee, had not anticipated the huge amount of electricity it took to make one short film.

The bar top held dozens of miniature green and

burgundy–colored crock bottles of wine samples. A salesman had given them to him in exchange for setting up a "date" with a friend of his. Augus sold the hundred forty-four little bottles of wine for two dollars apiece at the disco rent party. Just enough to pay his current long-distance phone bill.

Turning from the bar, I watched Augus glide over to his bed. His ivory body was scantily covered by a pair of purple and blue undershorts. His plump ass drooped out in ripples on its descent to his thighs. The "bed," which was a couch during business hours, was covered by a fur spread—genuine wolf and coyote pelts. That spread and his jewelry were the only remaining symbols of his grand past. "The rest escaped me quicker than cocaine." My anger was subsiding now that I had caught up with him.

"Why'd you leave me stranded at the Chelsea?"

"You aren't ever stranded, Lewis, my dear viper," he said quietly as he laid down on top of the fur. "Not as long as Uncle Woody is still smiling down upon you."

"Why'd you leave me?" I repeated, noting the bored look on his face.

"You don't remember, Lewis? You don't remember hitting me on my bare ass with my belt after you got tired of me and that pretty little girl we picked up at Ashley's? Everything was fine until I got lost in her," he said, spreading his legs out on that couch. Augus had long legs covered with golden hair. "At first I rather enjoyed your little ad-lib, but then I saw your face. You weren't acting. That little girl was shaking for an hour after I got her home. She said at first you spanking my ass excited her. Then she looked at your face. Said it reminded her of her mother once when she beat her with a coat hanger. She said she loved watching you make love to me. Liked your style, learned a lot. Didn't you hear her screaming?"

I thought back to the time before I awakened in that empty hotel room. I remembered.

"Why, Lewis?" he asked, holding up his arms for me to enter.

"I don't know," I said, crawling up from the end of that bed into his arms.

"I know you don't," he said. He pulled my face down beside his. "It's all right, baby," he whispered. "I know. Poppa knows, little girl."

ugus and I did bars on Mondays, if I could afford them. Monday was "our day." Monday was the day Augus made up to me for Saturday and Sunday, "his days." Our itinerary usually included a late breakfast, the last of his wonder weed, and a carefully designed tour of one of his New Yorks. I usually was panting like a teacup poodle by Monday. Kitty, if he knew, would usually tell me what Augus had done over the weekend. Kitty was Augus's East Side pit stop. "Baby, our baby's elbows and knees were raw. He worked this group of four last Saturday. Mother here," he'd said, "cleansed them with peroxide first. Then I applied some A&D ointment and kissettes. Didn't he tell you that story, Sugar? I always ask him to call you when he stops by here. I say, 'Gussy, give our angel a call. She's lying down there in her little apartment drink-ing and drop-ping Valium.' 'No!' Augus says. 'She needs the pain. Don't you know by now?' he says to me, 'She likes the pain. It's a pleasure to her.'"

All Augus would say to me about his weekends was that he was doing God's work. "Time for me to get on out there, Toots. Got to do God's work," he'd say. "What you gonna do while I'm at work?" he'd ask every Friday. "Valium," I usually answered, angry that he was leaving. Usually I pretended I was asleep before he left me. Some-times I'd call his answering service just to have something to do other than drink, cry, and sleep. Kitty said he called Augus's service, too, when he was lonely. "Sometimes," Kitty confessed, "I use my voices." How do you think he felt that first time the operator gave him messages from Lena Horne, Eartha Kitt, and Elizabeth Taylor?

Of the thousands of people my Checker cab must have passed as it raced down Fifth Avenue toward my apartment in Greenwich Village, I didn't notice one person until I was paying the driver at the corner of Washington Place and Sixth Avenue. There Augus was, sauntering up the street in front of O'Henry's. He took his glasses off when he saw me, blew on them, and deposited them in the pocket of his grayish corduroy suit that had been navy blue at one time. I hated that suit.

I wish I could say that was the reason he wore it so often, but it wasn't. The early seventies were a little rough on Augus's business ventures. "Threads of the past." That's what he called his worn clothing. Nobody could wear that suit but him, he said, because nobody but him knew where all the frayed seams were located. One could never consider bending over in it to tie a shoelace, for example, or lifting one's arm to signal a cab. He also had on his favorite antique Saint Laurent silk shirt and one of those wide plaid wool ties that he had favored since he lost his silk ones. In a New York sort of way, he managed to maintain a certain air of elegance, even at his lowest moments; he had the style even if he didn't have the stuff.

Just as I slammed the cab door, he reached me. Lifting his left index finger up to his lips to signal silence, he grabbed my right arm with his left hand and started pulling me down Washington Place toward my apartment. As we approached my black wrought-iron gate, he pulled out his keys and used them—something he had never done. Once inside my studio, he released his grip on me and headed toward my john. Before he could take refuge in the toilet, I got started.

"You cocksucking scumbag son of a bitch," was first. He took my attack in silence, just stood there by the john door wiping his glasses. When he got tired of listening, he put on his glasses and pushed me over to the bed, forcing me down with his legs, straddling me across my neck.

"I couldn't come up there, man. I just couldn't come. Hospitals make me sick. The thought of you locked in a psycho ward, man, that tore me up," he said, tears falling from him to me. "Why'd you have to throw that tantrum on the street? My neighbors said you couldn't be stopped. I've got to replace four plate-glass windows, man . . . Lewis, I wasn't home. I didn't call the police on you. I was out with Chocolate and the Pogo Stick, having a couple of laughs and a beer. Believe me."

As he finished he bent down to kiss me. That's when I butted him in the face with my head, breaking his glasses. "Oh, boy," he said, holding on to his bleeding nose. "These were the only ones I had left." That's when he got up and headed to the bathroom. "I can't seem to stop the hurt you feel. I try. I didn't start it." At this point the tears were flowing, mixing with the blood.

"I'll see you around, Toots," he said as he walked out the door. He was through the gate and gone before I could give him his glasses. It took me three months and two hundred and forty messages on his service to convince him to return my calls.

One Monday around noon I got this call from Augus. "I'm around the corner at the Pink Teacup. What do you want with your grits? Fried fish, fried chicken, or smothered pork chops?" Before I could answer, he responded, "I'll order one fish and one chicken." My nipples went erect just hearing his voice. "Don't start that dialogue about your hair. I gave you time to get ready, little girl. Didn't I? Okay!" he continued. "Wear that blue cotton shirtwaist dress and those high-heeled patent-leather pumps. Nothing else. You understand me? Nothing. Now, hurry up! I missed you, girl," he whispered. "Bring some change."

Augus opened the door of the Pink Teacup before I crossed the narrow Village street. "Hi, Toots," he said, appraising my appearance. "You cheated," he commented as he smelled behind my ear. "Smell good. That fragrance mixes well with this grease." He was leading us to "our" table, the one in the corner by the window. The second I sat down, I carefully crossed my feet at the ankles, anticipating his move. "Your food will be here in a second. I knew you'd be late. Can't you ever do exactly what I ask, man? You're thirty minutes late and you're wearing the wrong dress." Reaching down under the table, he slid his hands beneath my dress, stopping when he noted I'd obeyed one order. "Why a silk black dress with slits up the side?" he asked as he handed me a glass of wine. "I told you to wear that blue cotton."

"You can see through it in the sunlight," I said, sipping on my wine.

"That's why I chose it," he replied quietly. "I really like that effect on you."

After breakfast Augus began our tour. Today we walked across West Greenwich Village to the border of East Greenwich Village. We stopped at Washington Square Park to listen to some street music. Our trip ended at one of my favorite places, Lady Astor's.

"Go on in," he directed. "I've got a couple of other stops to make. It's four now. I'll meet you inside at six. Time you became more independent. Breakfast busted me; loan me forty-five." He waited patiently while I slipped the money out of my shoe. "When you get in there, sit at the bar like always. The bartender will take care of you. Every now and then give 'em a little thigh. Make 'em think they're gonna see it," he said, accepting my money. "See me, lady," he purred out as he discreetly enfolded me in his arms. "I'm tired of you staying home by yourself. I'm freezing you." As he talked, he took his fingertips and squeezed between my legs until he felt my thighs tighten. "A liberated wo-man can travel alone." I could feel it throb.

"I'm counting on you to take care of yourself. I betcha you won't have to buy a single drink for yourself," he said, unfolding me. "You can handle yourself. I do. I've been traveling without money, panties, and company for years now." Smiling gallantly with only his lips, he hailed a cab and left me.

SMOKE

They won, Woody. Wood-dee, they won." Even though I repeated this until my throat refused to make a fool of itself anymore, the ceiling did not seem to hear, just kept on looking blankly down at me. It knew, as I did, that we were alone. Woody had left with Sestra after I cut him on the back; that had really gotten Sestra disgusted at us because I'd done it with one of her favorite Baccarat stems. That was a waste of good glass to her—jelly glasses, a Welch's grape jelly glass would have done. I'd promised to calm down after he let me up off the floor. He kept on saying he didn't have any date with any "little pussy"; he was going over to a meeting at his friend Guy's place. I could call him over there in an hour if I didn't believe him. He was doing a fine job, too, until he went into his closet to change his clothes, a fine job until he took off his baby-blue cotton boxer shorts and went to replace them with a new pair of red polyester jockeys. Sestra shouldn't have smiled that smile at me, either, when she saw all of this. I tried to pour myself another glass of champagne, not see, but I couldn't. Before she could warn him, I broke the stem right off that sho' 'nuff real crystal glass that had been a wedding gift from Kitty-Kat and went for him. Just as he reached for his pants I landed on his back, scraping that stem from his right shoulder down to the left side of his waist. I don't think he knew what I'd done until Sestra ran up and threw my bedspread over me. Sestra said she thought she'd seen that scene in a movie before, that's how she knew what to do. They left, she said, because I promised to de-tit her completely and eat them as an appetizer to the entrée—his balls—if they did not leave "my house." Her offer to drive us downtown and help me to give him a hot Golden Shower in the middle of Woodward Avenue hadn't appealed to me at all. She'd laughed until she had to pee when she saw how much he enjoyed the pain he felt as she soaked his cuts in alcohol. "Pain is pleasure for some, Lewis."

I'd started the fire after I checked the garage for his Lotus. It was there, her Eldorado was gone. Freddie Lee got it first. He was a pink burlap wall hanging that I'd bought in Haiti. I started with his tail. Then my straw basket collection. After the cup of bacon grease got to going, I marched upstairs like one of Mary Shelley's monsters, locked my bedroom door, dimmed the lights, stretched out on our bed, and waited. I was trying my damnedest to look like Sleeping Beauty most of that time. Then I remembered Sestra had placed two more bottles of Cristal champagne in the freezer to chill right before the brawl. I'd about decided to run down and rescue them when I heard the first aerosol bottles explode. They sounded like two hundred pounds of popcorn popping. Then Smoke crept under my door and started his blabbering.

"Didja, Anna Lou? Wanna play with me? Where you be at, little girl? You did call. Didn't you, kiddo?" I didn't make a move. Maybe if I didn't say anything he'd think I was already gone. "Chile, I weren't looking for you jest yet. No sirree bob!"

"Woody, help me," I demanded as quietly as I could as I waited upon Smoke to find me. "Big girls need their daddies, too, huh?" Smoke said in reply. He was right up on me now.

"You let 'em touch me, Woody. You weren't supposed

to." I was squeezing my eyes tightly, whispering to Woody. "In sickness and in health, huh?" Smoke asked. "I'm your high-stepper, Woody?" Then the sirens; for the first time I heard them.

Sestra told me recently that I called her and told her about Smoke. She and Woody arrived seconds before the firemen, whom they'd called. "There I was, broad in my nightgown, my big ass hanging out, standing on your goddamned porch ringing your goddamned doorbell. Those fellas knocked in that glass door quicker than a whore could bat her artificial double lashes three times. I swear, bitch, I think you brought my menopause on that time."

When Smoke didn't say any more for a while, I opened my eyes to see if he'd perhaps taken me against my will. I was still in that room; I knew that because the first thing I saw was Woody's favorite Charles Cold painting—the bald head of a pink man who resembled Woody. He kept saying I'd adjust to it if I learned to appreciate the skill of the artist, his control of the palette, his strength. Asshole red is what I saw when I looked at it this time, too. Hatred of that painting gave me the strength to get up. One foot pulled me to the floor, the other one to that painting. From here my hands took over and did what my brain hadn't had the sense to do earlier. They yanked that monster off that wall, slid that window back, and threw him out of my bedroom. From out there I heard Woody. "She's alive! She's alive." There were Woody and Sestra and every last one of my neighbors standing outside my patio looking up at me. "Quit standing there looking like Quasimodo, shitface. Jump!" My toes twitched first, then my ankles, as I came back and realized that this was really me standing there wearing only a beige slip.

"Annie Lou, I'm still waiting," Smoke was yakking again right behind me. "Come on and play with me. You look like a high-wire artist, standing there like that. High Stepper, star for me. You want me standing up or lying down?" "I want you later," I screamed at him as my hands and feet took over again and threw me out of that window. I landed on top of Woody's bed of poppies.

PART TWO

CONNECT

BROOK

Sestra and I were in Woody's exercise room playing exercise when I told her about Brook. At first all she did was fidget with the white drawstring on her sweat suit and look at me. I remember wondering why she wasn't sweating like me.

"It sounds like bondage to me. I think you're in deep waters. I'd appreciate it if you'd keep me out of this one. You're used to being cared for, you like being number one. This one has to look out for himself first. That's how he lives. That's the only way he can live. It must be devastating for a man to know that even a small woman can beat him up. Ready for the steam room?" she asked, staring at me.

"Now that you've told me about him," Augus whispered on the telephone, "I'm gonna tell you about my two-hundred-fifty-pound lady. I just love burying myself in her platters of fat. Her body is so comfortable and warm. She can take my weight," he whispered cheerfully.

"Do you think he'll like me?" Kitty-Kat breathlessly asked. He was into one of his acts. "I do so want him to like me," he purred like Eartha Kitt. "Will he?" he demanded in a military voice. "Like me? Will I like him, Puddin'?"

"You'll love him, Poopsie-pie. He's everything you ever wanted in a man, too."

"Honey," he said, real Pearl Bailey like, "I'm about ready to settle for a head myself. These pretty young Puerto Ricans are increasing in cost like Texas beef. I tried out a closet drag queen the other night. She had smeared sardine oil on her twat to make her smell like an authentic girl. I was so desperate for something easy! I'm also bored with these flabby old men that decided to fly out of their closets in the seventies. They're creating an imbalance on the market."

"What I love about you, Lewis," Prince proclaimed, "is your sense of equality. You know that most men are inferior to you. Right, baby? Doesn't matter if the brother can walk or not. You want a piece of his mind. Ain't I right?"

"Naw," I said, real Southern. "I am in love. He's the first man I met who I feel is superior to me. Some of you are perhaps equal?"

Woody's bedroom was a section of his side of the apartment that I usually tried to avoid after we divorced. It contained such relics as his customized Japanese bike, which hung on the wall; the steering wheel to his first sports car, a 1949 Alfa Romeo; an antique wooden airplane propeller; and a collection of African masks. This blissful morning I was so excited I didn't even notice he was asleep.

"Woody, Woody!" I cried out as I entered right before dawn. "I've found him, I have truly found him this time." As I repeated myself I dropped my dress, my panties, and my shoes beside his four-poster bed.

"Tell me all about it later," he drowsily pleaded. "Cookie just left here. All she talked about all night was not finding him in me." I slid my backside into his arms. I was so filled with finding him that I didn't get angry at smelling her on my pillow. Woody's rotund, hairy belly felt like home to my soft behind.

"This time it's serious. I have really found him. He's everything I ever wanted."

"Rich, huh?"

"Not in dollars!"

"Tall?"

"Yes!"

"Handsome?"

"Very!" I pictured him lying on his hundreds of pillows, his long black hair sprawled against them.

"Rich?" he repeated softly.

"In manners and culture," I replied quickly.

"Poor!" he stated, feigning disappointment.

"He wouldn't be if he weren't paralyzed."

"Paralyzed? Which half?"

"Both. Got his neck broken in a prep school wrestling match when he was eighteen." I shuddered, hearing his neck snap.

"You've got real problems, Lewis," Woody whispered as he dozed off. "You really know no boundaries, do you?"

"He's majestic," I said, thinking of the way he sat up so straight in his chair.

"He's a quadriplegic," he said. "And I'm asleep, Lewis. Quiet." With this he fell into a soft snore.

I turned over in his arms and faced him. Woody was aging. By the soft dawn light that filtered through his window, I studied his face resting on my bare chest. The smooth olive skin had retained its patina. It was the tone around his eyes that was different. The aquiline nose that I'd once had ambitions of having surgically copied for my own face had two dark marks across its bridge from his glasses. One extra-long coarse black hair hung out of the right nostril. I'd cut it in the morning. The heavy black and gray mustache and sideburns were too bushy.

As I studied Woody, I began to drift. I remembered Brook and all of last night. And the man who had no legs that my little sister, Kark, and I used to run from in cold fright. I wondered how he felt watching stupid little children run from him as he approached them perched on his homemade skate box. Or had he gotten over all that, along with the rest of the things like having to look up at almost everyone over three feet tall? My mother told us that we should be whipped for all that screaming and running we'd do each time we saw that po' man coming down the street as best he could on his way to the store.

I could hear Brook as clearly as if he were on the other side of me, talking to me in that melodic Southern accent of his as we flowed into each other. "LeeAnn should not have disturbed you. I told her to go on to that dinner party with Barry and not worry about me." Burned his feet, it seemed, trying to handle the hot water spout on his urn. At least he thought he had burned them. That water certainly was steaming. He'd needed LeeAnn to take off his boots for him so that he could see for himself. Three of the toes on his right foot were burned about second degree. She'd wrapped them in gauze and medicated petroleum jelly. I unwrapped them, gave them a kiss and air. His feet were snake-belly white, swollen, and soft as a baby's; twenty years of no use. Tiny sea-blue veins crisscrossed his instep, looped around his ankles, and then disappeared into a bush of coarse dark hairs. I could still feel those hairs on my thighs. "Follow me," he'd directed. "Listen to my music, woman. Give you to me."

"Woody's my ex-husband," I reheard myself explain to him. "We're divorced, two years now."

"Not separated yet?"

"Kitty's this homosexual friend that I live with in New York. We've thought about having a baby one day. Kitty's so pretty and so funny."

"I bet," he responded, smiling.

Rose, Woody's Jamaican housekeeper, was preparing his breakfast by the time I awakened and came into the kitchen. He was finishing the sports section as I plopped down at the table breathlessly.

"Won't you let me tell you even now?" I asked, accepting a glass of carrot juice from Rose.

"As soon as I read *B.C.*," he promised, folding back the page. "Wanna know what your horoscope predicts this morning, July 25, 1977?" Then without waiting: "Capricorn beware! Guard natural instincts to accept extreme challenges."

"He's a Libra. Read his," I suggested.

"Do look that gift goat in the mouth!"

"Good thing you're an allergist instead of an astrologist."

"What's his name?" he asked, dipping a tablespoon of peanut butter into his bowl of shredded wheat and milk. I never knew anyone to eat shredded wheat and peanut butter before Woody. He swore by it for energy.

"Brook Fields," I said, seeing him smile again as I straddled his chest.

"Sounds like an actor."

"A textbook writer. He had planned on becoming an admiral before the accident." I heard his neck snap, saw him fall, lying on that gymnasium floor thrashing like a chicken whose head had just been wrung.

"I'll treat you guys to dinner this week," Woody said, beginning his poached eggs and English muffins. I had long ago promised Woody that I would never select another man for myself. According to him, I had atrocious taste in men.

"I love you the best, Woody," I said as I began my breakfast.

"I love you too, baby," he said, finishing his. "Got to run. Monday's a heavy one for the allergy crowd. My junkies need their fix." With this he rose, smiling. Woody always smiled and opened his arms for me. "Good luck, sweetie pie," he said as I walked into them. "He's gonna be tough."

S he there yet?" I whispered into the phone.

"Who?" he asked, sounding very nasal.

"Your helper." I was sure he told me she arrived promptly at eight. That's why I had to hurry and leave, he'd said.

"Not yet. She doesn't arrive until ten."

"How'd you like to go on a picnic today?" I tried to soften my voice and emphasize my Southern accent as I talked.

"Sounds great. I haven't been on a picnic in two years. I can be ready by one. Gotta go now, I think I hear her coming." It was ten-thirty exactly. "We've got a pressing matter to take care of over here today. See you at one, Lewis."

I worked on myself for the next two hours, drank two glasses of prune juice so I could be a pound slimmer by the time I left for his house. I shaved everywhere, bleached my mustache, bathed in Dr. Pryor's Jinx Removing Crystals, and prayed. I put on one of my most feminine dresses, a blue cotton peasant dress with a smocked bodice; white mule sandals adorned freshly scrubbed and painted toes. I felt high as I packed an insulated bag full of Woody's favorite beer, John Courage.

Walking out into the sunshine, I felt young and weightless for the first time in a year. "At last, at last, at last," I kept repeating as I drove across town.

His door was open when I arrived. I dashed through it like Loretta Young. There my love sat reading a book, waiting, all scrubbed himself. "You smell like an herb garden," he said. Good boy, I thought. He recognizes the lavender oil. "We're going on a picnic?"

"For sure. My type," I said, walking over to kiss him. "You comb your hair yourself?" I asked as I bent down. It was all mussed up to look natural.

"Let's say I rearranged it. My helper, Mrs. Richards, always tries to eliminate my natural curl. But I always fix it when she leaves," he said, smiling like a naughty boy.

———

"Please, get my sun hat out of the closet for me. It's the Van Gogh. I purchased it in Italy when I was traveling." He looked so dramatic in it. The whole scene didn't seem real.

As we proceeded to try to leave his apartment, I saw for the first time how damaged he was. He couldn't roll his chair over the threshold without great effort. Soon as I can, I vowed silently, I'm going to grab that chair and push it. He really can't, I thought.

"Okay," he panted out, rolling over his threshold. "Sometimes I feel as if I'm crawling around on my belly, man. Before we can lock this door, you'll have to get the key. It's in that pink and green ceramic mug in my study, the one attached to the shortest wooden handle." The handles made it possible for him to open doors, I learned.

Sliding past him into his den, I saw a beautiful cup containing three keys with special wooden handles. I picked out the shortest one.

"Was that your mother's picture? It looks just like old pictures of my mother," I said, returning. She was very fair, keen-featured with long, stringy brown hair. She wore one of those wide-shouldered, sequin-trimmed dresses so popular during the forties. "Pretty lady," I said as I locked his door.

"She was a good lady," he said. "She took care of me for five years after I was injured. She wouldn't let anyone but my father touch me if she could help it. She was never the same after I was hurt. My accident weakened her. I think it killed her," he said, looking up at me. "Say, how about holding my head back so I can straighten myself up? Just place the palm of your hand on my forehead. That's it," he said slowly, using my hand to straighten his body up in his chair. "I look like a duck waddling, don't I?" he asked, wiggling himself straight. He did.

"Nope," I lied, taking my hand away. I could feel the indentations in his forehead where so many hands had been placed earlier.

"Would you mind checking to see if that thing is securely placed in my boot?" he asked. The tube was in his boot.

"It's secure, Captain," I responded, checking his boot. They were made of fine black leather, spit-shined.

"Good! Now, if you will pull my pants leg down, we can proceed. Pull them down from my thighs. That's real good," he said as I tugged at his starched, bleached-out jeans. "I'm into aesthetics," he said as I walked to the back of his chair and began pushing him down the hall. "I learned through these years that my public prefers the gory details of my life be kept to myself."

"Why don't you get an electric one?" I asked, trying to catch my breath.

"I've worn out three. I can't afford one right now. They cost as much as a good, small used car."

"You've got to back your car out," he instructed as I pushed him near Woody's slick beige Cadillac. "I have to be parallel to the door first. We'll use this board here as a slide." We slid him into the car by his will and my body with hardly any trouble. "It's all in the movement," he told me after he was transferred. "You've got good movement. Do you dance?" I had good movement!

I headed straight for the Eastern Market. London has Convent Gardens, Manhattan has Balducci's, Detroit has the Eastern Market. Brook leaned back on the beige leather upholstery, wearing the straw hat and sucking up my soul and the sights along the way.

"Your car is really nice," he said, turning to look at me. "I've never owned a car."

"Me either, this is my ex-husband's." The market area was peaceful, quiet by this time. I performed the entire scene for his amusement. Quick stop at the Hirt Co. for cheese, crackers, churned butter, and a new basket. Then Gabriel's Middle Eastern Imports for six different kinds of olives and pita bread. Then the Gratiot Central Market for the appetizer, kosher corned beef sandwiches on rye and Vernor's ginger ale.

"I just adore this area of town," I said as I placed half the hot corned beef on the top of his hand. This is how he held sandwiches. "Woody's building is right over there," I said, pointing toward the east. "I'm his only tenant. He has an office downstairs," I said, digging into my sandwich. "This stained-glass artist designed these windows for him. You can see the geisha that she made for my bedroom windows from the street. I'll show you. Woody had her do a smiling Buddha for his bathroom window."

"Is there an elevator?" he asked, catching mustard in his beard.

"No!" I said.

"Then the only way I'll get to see it is from the street. I quit allowing myself to be carried up over two steps after thirty-five," he stated, indicating by his eyes that he was ready for the rest of his sandwich. By the time I parked near the Scott Fountain at Belle Isle, I was committed to him for life.

We got out of the car by sliding in the opposite direction. The only change was that this time I had to reassemble his chair. He carried his basket on board. The only moment he hesitated to do everything I wanted came when

I flagged down two young Detroiters to ask them to help me get him on the ground. Later he told me that he was afraid he'd have to tell them about his hose. He didn't wish to embarrass them. Men found the hose part especially difficult to deal with, he explained.

"Been in Nam, bro?" asked one of the fellas helping Brook to the ground. "I made that scene."

"No, I missed that," Brook responded with an uneasy smile. "Thanks a lot," he said, resting on these quilted blankets I had on the ground.

"How about a beer?" I asked, reaching into the bag. "Just getting off work?" I asked, noticing their U.S. Rubber badges.

"Just getting ready to go," one said, smiling, flashing me a doobie in the palm of his hand. "Came out to the island to cool out. The trees and water calm me."

"Thanks," the other one said as I handed him a beer. He was staring at Brook's tube, which was dangling out of his boot. "Y'all brother and sister?" he asked, looking at me to see if I saw. "You look a lot alike."

"Yeah," I responded before Brook tried to explain. "Thanks so much," I said as they left.

"I haven't touched the ground in two years. My second wife, Royale, and I brought Circe out here for her birthday. Circe was her little girl. We married when she was one. I miss the child more than I do the mother."

"You want another baby?"

"More than I want to walk. That's out for me, you know. My seeds are locked up inside my body," he revealed. "Kind of like a woman's, I guess," he said, accepting a beer from me.

S he's coming, she's coming," Brook yelled out in his sleep. Opening his eyes, he softly started to repeat himself. Embarrassed, he stopped, cleared his throat. "It's time for you to leave. My nurse is on her way. I . . . I try to keep her out of my personal business." By this time I was crawling off the end of his bed, frantically reaching for my underclothes that reclined on his chair like a limp Dalí watch. My heart pounded in my chest as I frantically covered my body, racing against time. She was coming! I was feeling like a welfare father must feel right before he jumps into his woman's closet.

Y ou got any more of that stuff?" Brook asked, holding on to his chair arms as he checked his wall of windows. No neighbor was peeping at us. "That stuff" was waiting patiently on a hand mirror on the dining table.

"Want some more?" I asked, rising from his couch. "Take it from the foil. There isn't very much," I said, placing the foil beneath his nose. I vowed not to give him the stash I had in a tiny glass vial in my robe pocket. Not tonight, anyway. He vacuumed all that stuff up before I had a chance to change nostrils. Not a granule was left for a freeze for me.

"Wee," he said, throwing his head back as far as he could manage. "Wow! I wish they'd sell this like they sell vitamins. I think I need it. Didn't you want any?" he asked as he brought his head forward. "It'd mess with your vodka, I bet," he said, watching me examine the mirror. "Lewis, you've done it again. Yes, you certainly have."

"Got you high?"

"That, too! Introduced me to another woman that I really, really do like." This will make number three, I thought as I sat back on his couch.

"Really?" I asked, trying not to look too astonished. He'd promised not to pick anyone I knew again after the last time. The last time a young friend had asked me to ask him not to call anymore. Her woman had gotten really upset over Brook's calls. She'd called him a frustrated eunuch, pulled a knife on my young friend. I'd told him all about it.

"Who is it this time?"

"I'm not going to tell you this time," he said, dropping his right leg down off his pedal so that he could void. "You won't chase this one away with your horror stories." I'd told the first one about the kind of help he demanded from me. "I know you intend to be the only queen on this chessboard. I'm not gonna tell you ever. No, man, not me!" he emphasized, winking at me. "You might get angry at her and tell her again. She's just my type, soft, satiny, and . . ." he listed.

"Silent, selfish, and poor," I added, pulling out my tiny vial filled with another girl he liked. "Want some?" I asked, walking toward his chair.

"You really think you know me, don't you?" he asked as I stuck that vial up into his left nostril.

"Yeah, I do," I said as he inhaled her.

Woody," I whispered into the telephone. "It's me, the sissy."

"I know your voice by now, Lewis. What's up?"

"That's the problem—nothing," I whispered.

You tell her about me, Lewis. You know what to say. I'm tired of explaining myself to people," Brook said over one of those eternal cups of tea. "One day I'm going to write a pamphlet, entitle it 'Brook the Quad,' and place it right outside my door in one of those little boxes that say *Take One*. The introductory paragraph will begin, 'I'm Brook Fields. I'm paralyzed from the shoulders down to the tips of my big toes. I've been rehabilitated to the extent that I even pay taxes.' Then it'll go something like this," he said, using a child-like voice. "'I can talk.'" He pointed to his mouth. "'I can see.'" He stretched his eyes. "'I can hear.'" He wiggled his ears. "'I can undress myself if,'" he whispered, "'you give me a lot of time, but,'" his voice dropped lower, "'I can't dress myself. I can't sh-h-h'"—he stopped here and flopped his head down—"'myself if.' Please, Lewis. Give her all of the details for me. If you think she isn't strong enough to handle all of them, give her bus fare and my sincere thanks," he said, slamming his mug onto his board.

"No problem," I said, rising from my chair. "Gimme a kiss and I won't tell her about your morning breath." He didn't like to kiss me anymore, but he did. "Wowee, that, sir, had enough zam to make me want to apply for the job myself. Why not hire me?" I asked, headed for the kitchen. "I'm strong enough."

"That wouldn't work, my dear. Last night your martinis inspired one of your most interesting harangues. Right before you passed out, you told me that you intended to be the only queen on my chessboard." I didn't remember any of that. "I can see it all now. 'Hello, Dr. Fields's residence. Is this Elly Mae? No? You sound just like another friend of his. Her name is Elly Mae. She calls him about this time every day when I'm at my busiest.'"

"I wouldn't."

"Yes, you would. Let's keep our thing friendly. Okay?"

"I'll interview her with you. If you don't want her, signal me by asking her if she'd like a cup of coffee," I said, handing him another cup of tea. "If you want her, I'll tell her all about the effects of your paralysis during her ride home."

"True touch and all?" he asked, smiling.

"True touch and all," I responded.

We were exactly seven days old as "friends." It was one of the few lazy Sundays we ever spent together. The night before, Kitty had arrived in town and bopped over to meet The Head, as he secretly called Brook. Everybody always loves Kitty at first sight. Brook did. Everything had gone fine until we got wrecked on Kitty's specialty—champagne and cognac combined. Kitty in a creative stupor had baked a spinach soufflé for us. And he had reenacted several "sexette" encounters for us. Including the one where he picked up a karate expert that enjoyed brutality before "he gave himself to me." Seems like Kitty ended up running wildly down the hall naked, screaming, after the first chop.

Everything was perfect until it was time for K-K to leave. As I walked him to the door, K-K suddenly pranced back into the living room and grabbed Brook in an embrace that ended up in a kiss. Any man that allowed K-K's lips on him for longer than ten seconds was classified as a "possibility." It took Brook almost fifteen seconds to break that kiss. I later tried to explain to K-K that it was shock and physical difficulty that pushed him over the ten-second limit. Kitty said Brook went over the limit because he enjoyed it. Brook said nothing about it that night or ever.

Waking that Sunday morning, lying in that bed with my mouth glued under his armpits, I felt as if I'd found home. His armpits smelled like lilacs to me. I found myself nibbling on his long hairs. I wanted to take him everywhere. In all of my life, I had never wakened before with a man whom I wished to explore.

"Morning, Lewis," he murmured in a nasal voice. "I'm still really tired." I was lapping at his armpits at the time. I'd just felt her harden. "I've got to get up, got a deadline to make on a *Smithsonian* article. Stop that now." Reluctantly I released him, leaping out of bed as quickly as I could. When I neared his stomach, I expertly reached under the covers and grabbed his full chrome urinal from between his legs.

"Be right back," I promised. As I was replacing it, he reached up and grabbed at my snatch, which was peeping out from beneath one of his gigantic pajama tops. Automatically, I responded by recoiling.

"Don't like it unless you're directing, huh? Excuse me." With this he began hitting himself lightly on his kidney area the way he did when he felt he should void.

"An arm's distance away from me is sometimes too distant," he said at the ceiling.

hoped I was the only one that could smell the urine on us as I pulled up in Joe Muer's restaurant lot and parked by the attendants' little shed. We simply didn't have time to go back to his apartment and start all over again. It'd been my fault. I should have checked that damn clasp before I helped Brook into the car. Brook was meeting Woody for the first time. We hadn't even discussed going back inside to start over again. "How you doing, ma'am?" Lamont, the smiling attendant, asked as he came up to my door.

"Fine, fine, Lamont," I replied, sliding out of the door. Lamont smelled it. "Please give my friend a hand. He has a chair in the trunk." Brook was looking at us, smiling. He cheerfully waved at Lamont. Lamont smiled.

"Sure, ma'am," he said enthusiastically, going around to the trunk, which I'd popped from the inside.

"We're meeting the doctor," I said, lifting the frame of the chair out of the trunk. "Have you seen him?"

"Not yet. How you doing, sir?" he asked, graciously rolling the chair up to the back door for Brook.

"Very well," Brook said, "under the circumstances. Could you give me a hand here?" he asked, looking up at Lamont standing there. "I'll need to stop at the men's room before I go in for dinner. Had an accident."

"Certainly. My pleasure."

"You from Kentucky or Tennessee?" Brook asked while Lamont placed the board expertly under Brook's hips.

"Lexington, sir. Been up here half my life."

"I'm from Hartsville, Tennessee, myself."

"How'd you tell? My accent?"

"That and your manners," Brook said real Southern-like. Lamont was bent down, holding him by his belt, ready to begin Brook's ascent out of that car.

Just as Lamont got Brook into his chair, Woody and Cookie arrived. I was all ready to say, "There's Woody," when Brook whistled long and low. "There's a man of fine taste," he said softly, staring at Woody's car, a canary-yellow Lotus Elan.

"That's the doctor," Lamont said, running over to open the door for Woody.

"That's Woody?" Brook asked.

"And his woman," I said quietly, watching as Cookie lightly bounced out with Lamont's help.

Help me make a baby tonight?"

"You've got the wrong fella here, Lewis," Woody said, mixing himself a fresh drink.

"Please?"

"For you and Brook?"

"Me and Brook." He was handing me a fresh drink now. Vodka on the rocks.

"Check out those test tubes."

"I already did." I finished my drink.

"And?" He finished his drink and collected my empty glass before he headed for the bottles again.

"They don't take single women."

"So, get married. You're both single." On the rocks for both of us this time.

"He says he wants a baby, not me."

"Umm!"

Honey, it amazes me how much time each of us puts in and the work never seems to end," Mrs. Richards whispered to me as I stood slushing a cup of tea down and a freshly baked bran muffin. "Lewis, why don't you sit down and enjoy your breakfast?"

"Can't. I've got to get him to his therapist by ten o'clock. It's eight-thirty now. He's really irritable this morning. Seems Doll can't get here to type until next week," I said, finishing my muffin. "Says he would fire her just on her attitude if he could find another typist as good as she is." Doll, I mused, had recently refused to help Brook get out of bed. "'I'm not going to get into your personal problems, Brook,' that witch said, standing there at the door, looking at me lying there," Brook told me.

Doll's attitude as expressed to me was that she knew her role. "I've got Vegas, he's the only baby I can handle. I'm clerical, not nursing. I ain't his woman. He says you aren't, either, nor Tommie," she had said with her elfin smile. Doll had the prettiest teeth. "You two obviously have nothing else to do but cuddle him. I have. Y'all like him. I don't. Admire, yes—like, no," she said peering at me from over her horn-rimmed glasses. She had small brown eyes that twinkled. "I think of him as simply a dude that ended up in a wheelchair. He play some real tough games. Even Mrs. Richards is taken in by him. She thinks he's helpless, too. Y'all just met him. What do you think he did those other nineteen years?" she asked. "He left home five years after the accident. Let's see, he's been married twice for a total of six years. The first one was a tobacco heiress, you know," Doll had said, staring at me.

"He had a fellowship to study in England," I said. "He didn't need her money." I was proud to be able to defend him on one count.

"He did, he did, but he needed some loving feet and hands. The kind of help he need money can't buy. She was his companion, typist, nurse, and driver. Furnished the extras, too." Doll was sharing one of her lists with me.

"Extras? Like what?" I asked, backing out of the office where we were chatting.

"Extras, you know, little lovings, theater tickets, fancy restaurants, country inns," she listed. "Clothes. Have you checked out some of those old classics of his? You just think you're the first one to insist that he get a suit custom-made. Some of his were made on Savile Row. Check his labels. He's in work clothes now because they suit his present posture."

"I better get back in there before he hollers. Thanks for the bite, Mrs. Richards," I whispered, turning to leave the kitchen. Brook was lying there swathed down in two baby-blue bath sheets. He cut Donahue off as I pulled back one of the towels. His body was hot to my touch. The temperature in his bedroom was usually eighty or eighty-five degrees.

Brook's body was always room temperature. He imagined how it felt from the neck down. I stood in front of him and slowly unbuttoned the shirt of his I wore. Underneath I wore a sheer blue pajama top. He smiled as he focused on my breasts. "Ready?" I asked, placing a black acrylic sock on one of his feet.

"More than ready. I thought you and Mrs. Richards were having high tea. Lewis, I'd prefer you to keep a certain distance from my helpers. Follow my example. I need privacy," he said. I slid a fresh green undershirt over his head while he talked, lifted one arm, pulled it through, then the other.

"I'll try," I promised, pulling his T-shirt down. "Jeans or cords today?"

"Wardrobe is your department. I've got too many other concerns today." With this he threw himself back on his pillows. I approached him from the foot of the bed with a pair of dark brown cords. Going around to the side, I placed my right leg up on his bed, preparing to slide his pants on. As I lifted his legs across mine, he hollered, "For Peter's sake, Lewis, be careful! Can't you see I'm voiding? I don't want that stuff backing up on me. My skin can't take it!" he screamed.

Before I could stop myself, I reacted by removing my leg and my hands. His legs dropped with a thud. "I'm doing the best I can!" I shouted as his body went into a spasm from the abrupt change. I saw Doll smiling.

"If this is your best this morning, then quit!" he demanded. "Mrs. Richards!" he screamed. "Mrs. Richards, come and give me a hand!"

You look like someone in one of those magazines. Long white scarf, riding boots, those dogs," Brook said as I got into Woody's car with them.

"Really? Which ones?"

"Oh, ah, one of the better ones."

"Not *Easy Rider*?" I subscribed to that one.

"Nope."

"Nor *Iron Horse*," Woody piped in as he started the car. We were going to the London Chop House for Valentine's Day. I was their guest.

"Nope," Brook responded. "I don't think I meant an American one at all. I think I meant one I've seen in London."

"Or Paris," Woody added.

"Right," he agreed.

"Wait until you see Long Tall Sally, man," Woody contributed.

"Long Tall Sally was a-walking through the alley," I sang out. "She's this waitress Woody loves to sneak looks at at the Chop House."

"That's right," Woody said, driving up to the restaurant. "She's the reason I come here whenever I have an extra hundred." I could see Brook now, watching her, thinking of how that long red hair would feel sliding across his chest. I hated her. Thinking of that bush of angel hair covering his mouth, I remembered that time he asked me not to trim mine. Remembered how embarrassed he looked when I told him I hadn't.

"I've got it now," he said as the doorman opened Woody's door. "You look like you came out of *Elle* magazine."

"Is that a good one, Woody?" I asked.

"One of the better ones," Woody responded, smiling.

Brook was very fond of drinking warm imported beer through a straw. The straw took the worry out of dropping the bottle. We were parked on this particular August afternoon in Memorial Park, which is very close to the Whittier Hotel. The Whittier is one of those rare relics left from the pretax era that features such luxuries as a private boat dock and an Olympic-size swimming pool with a fountain in the middle. It doesn't even take a keen imagination to envision Henry Ford I or Horace Dodge passing through for dinner. I had stopped there because it was now rare for anyone to dock there or park there anymore. Few people even knew about it. Woody had discovered it one day years ago when he'd had a boat.

Just as I was about to serve our bag lunch, this sail-boat appeared out of the Detroit River. "My, oh my," Brook commented. I decided to wait awhile before I told him it was Woody's old boat. Just as Brook got over the surprise of the boat, he was treated to a second pleasure: a six-foot female sailor wearing a red string bikini at the wheel. I decided to let him enjoy her before he received his next treat—Robinson Lexington Robertson III. As the girl cut the motor, Robin came up out of the galley wearing a matching red string bikini. Brook kept saying, "Jesus." I kept looking, waiting to tell him about them.

"Wonder what kind of ship is that?" he asked, still staring at her.

"A Swan 44," I professionally responded.

"How'd you know that?" he asked, staring at Robin as he jumped off the boat to tie it to the dock.

"Woody sold it to Robin, that guy there," I said just as Robin recognized me and waved slightly. He looked even better than he had the last time I saw him—thinner, darker, blonder. Looked like he had bleached his natu-rally sandy hair. This new version of him looked like it had come out of *Blue Boy*. Brook noticed immediately what I was focused on.

"Wonder how he managed to get that coconut inside of those teeny little trunks. Friend of yours?"

"Used to be."

"Know the woman, too?"

"Ummm. Yes. The type. He always has one of those types."

"What type is she?"

"Rich. Freak."

"Sounds like a winning combination to me."

"It sure is." I flashed back upon the one Robin had insisted I meet. Nina was northern Italian, blond. Everything had gone well until I awakened sober one morning to find her nestled up to my chest, suckling. I turned into Queen Kong before I knew it and threw her up against his wall. The thrust was so powerful that she was knocked unconscious. They told me later that she had suffered a brain concussion that affected her speech. From that moment on, she couldn't make clear *sh* sounds. Can you imagine what it must be like not to be able to say *shit* clearly? Robin had banned me from his private life as a result.

I was passing Brook one of the corned beef sandwiches when they climbed through the hatch onto the bow. She stared at our car momentarily before she slowly unfastened her top and laid down. Brook nearly choked on his sandwich. I kept my eyes on Robin, waiting for that satanic smile I'd seen appear right before one or another of the scenes he had created. He gave it to me right before he laid down on top of her. Brook turned slightly red as he realized what was happening on that bow. However, he never turned away. When Robin threw the bottom part of her bikini up in the air, I thought Brook's heart had stopped, he drew his breath in so sharply. I smiled now, remembering the time I'd gone out to dinner with Robin on a dare in Montreal wearing only a yellow lace minidress and a pair of matching yellow lace panties. It was amazing how many people appeared not to notice.

"They haven't made a sound," Brook whispered, as if we were in a theater.

"She will when he gives her the popper." As if he had heard me and obeyed, she began to make sounds that we could hear. I felt a tightening in my panties just before she let out one loud "Oh!" Brook dropped the last little piece of his sandwich.

"Where does he find them?" Brook asked. "I wanna go there, too."

"He doesn't," I responded, trying to decide if I should applaud or whistle or leave.

"They find him?"

"Sure do," I answered, turning on the motor one second before Robin rolled over, playing asleep.

"Wait just a second. Slow down, Lewis. I don't think the show's over," Brook said, staring ahead. It wasn't. Slowly she got up, slowly she turned around, and slowly she climbed down into the hatch.

"We can go now," Brook said, turning to me for the first time in what seemed like hours.

"Where to?"

"Oh, just drop me and my chair off wherever you think someone like that will find me. Some of them must enjoy steel and rubber."

"They do." And slavery, I thought, as I wiped the crumbs out of his mustache and beard.

Oh Baby and I would sometimes lie in my bed and play. We'd conjure Brook up and make him do whatever we wanted. Usually, after he appeared, we'd make him come up really close and look at our little girl. Sometimes his professional stare made us laugh at him. "Looks like a cornucopia," we made him say sometimes. "Let me fill her up for you ladies. Open up!" Then he'd touch our precious petal around the edges, tasting every now and then. "Tastes better than fresh black truffles, girls," he'd say. "So very, very sweet. It *is* mine, isn't it?" he'd ask. "Yours," we'd murmur back as his caresses made her nectar flow slowly down and out and over the edges. Then we'd make him leave, usually by the window, right before I disconnected her.

knew the girl coming out of the fire exit door was Brook's "friend" Tommie. She knew I was me, too, coming in that door. After sharing pillows, a woman can smell the other woman sight unseen. She knew Woody's car, I'm sure, as I knew hers. I'd guessed that she was a small one by the size of the terry cloth slippers she kept under Brook's bed. I'm sure she knew I was a big one by the size of the change of clothes that I kept in his closet. We didn't know the sound of each other's voice; Brook always answered his own phone. He didn't want Royale, his estranged wife, to know that either one of us "assisted" him, you see. This feigned state of help-lessness on his part brought the best out in most women. I'd had myself believing at the beginning that no one but me could take care of him. The part-time housekeeper was for keeping the house. Tommie was a friend. Sestra pulled my coat. "Dumb bitch," she had called me.

Tommie was copper-colored, tall and petite. She looked like one of those Yoruba art pieces from Nigeria. Her protruding, oily lips pouted just a little. Brown oval-shaped eyes full of green flecks darted out at the world. She made up in that little-makeup look some women master. Finely penciled charcoal lines emphasized the doe-like quality of her eyes. Rose tint accented her high, bony cheekbones. I knew her hairdo was his idea. Her dark, kinky hair was plaited geometrically around her small, sculptured head. The smallest pearl earrings you have ever seen pierced her ears. I was sure he had selected those, too. A properly used Burberry coat was wrapped nonchalantly around her. Aged Levi's fell correctly to the tips of well-used western boots. His long wool Van-derbilt scarf hung casually around her shoulders. As I approached the door, she dropped her eyes. But, alas, I had already caught her checking my hat. I had on an old green felt hat of his. She'd had to remove it too often not to have recognized it. As we carefully slid past each other, I caught her scent. Cocoa butter and roses. She smelled just like him. I kept tiny rose potpourri pinned inside of his pillowcases. I wanted to say hello, but I didn't. Isn't it strange how a man can separate women who might make good friends without him?

"She says you intimidate her," Brook had told me one night.

"How's that?" I had responded. "We've never met."

"Oh, she's heard about you," he had said.

"From whom, may I ask?"

I felt weighty and sluggish as I approached his door, just remembering her youthful sprightliness.

Brook was in the kitchen, trying vainly to place her favorite wineglass into the sink when I entered. I walked over and casually released his index finger from the stem of her glass. "May I have a glass of Spumante, too?"

"Sure," he said quietly, staring up at me. The pinkness of his cheeks showed his embarrassment. He liked me to think that all they ever did together was her homework or chat about his latest project over tea. Their relationship was casual, platonic, innocent, just like ours. We were only his friends.

"I ran into Tommie in the lobby." I was pouring myself the rest of their Spumante into a beer mug now.

"She stopped by on her way to her ballet class," he said, pulling at the crooked fingers of his left hand with the crooked fingers of his right hand. "She's been lifting weights trying to strengthen her back and arms," he said. "She says she hopes to have total command of her mind and body by the time she's twenty-three." He was patiently watching me gulp down that wine and then I lit up a cigarette.

"Why can't we officially meet?"

"She says she doesn't care to meet you," he said, breathing deeply between each word.

"Why's that, baby? Something she heard?"

"No, not something she's heard," he said, still pulling on his fingers. "Things she's seen."

"Like what?" I asked, walking out of his kitchen.

"Oh, that monstrous beige Cadillac of yours."

"That's not mine. That's Woody's," I yelled back from the bathroom. I wanted to check to see if she'd used her toothbrush recently. She had. Examining the two damp washcloths with my nose, I smelled her on one of them. Two kinky dark hairs were stuck to one of the towels, too.

"She knows that bottle of perfume up there isn't mine," he said, rolling up behind me just as I threw the used linens into his hamper. "And she can't help but notice that black silk kimono behind the door. She also knows that I don't use those Norforms that you insist upon leaving tucked in that drawer with my surgical supplies. I got a long lecture on endangered animal species when she saw your wolf coat in my closet. She also knows," he went on, "that I never sleep on the side of the bed where you insist upon leaving your glass."

"What else does she know?" I asked, putting up clean towels on his rack.

"She knows that you are one of my friends, too," he said, rolling out of the bathroom doorway.

"So why won't she meet me?"

"She doesn't feel that your style and her style would mix well. She's very quiet. She's a very private person," he mumbled as he went toward his bedroom.

"Lewis, please," he hollered out. "There is no contest. There is nothing to possess here. She understands that. She knows. You don't seem to understand that."

Brook and I had a lot of fun, especially on those long, cold, snowy Michigan Saturday afternoons. Mrs. Richards didn't come in on the weekends, which meant hard work for me but freedom for us. Sometimes he didn't get out of bed at all. This one Saturday I lay on my side of the bed reading *The Portrait of a Lady*. He was on his, reading *The Americans*. Henry James was our favorite. For quite a while I'd had thoughts of introducing Brook to my friend Oh Baby when the right moment came. The titles of our books must have been what inspired me to do it right then. She waited patiently under his bed, hidden in a plastic bag.

"Wanna meet Oh Baby?" I asked in about the same tone I'd use to ask, Wanna meet my mother?

"Oh who?" he asked, looking over at me.

"Oh Baby, my Japanese vibrator." At this I reached down and pulled her out.

"Looks like a little miniature tire to me," he said, staring at her. "I thought they were all shaped like bananas."

"My first ones were. I prefer her cute little shape to theirs. Woody gave me this and a box of firecrackers last Fourth of July. He gave his girl, Cookie, one too."

"Take the weight off himself a bit, huh?" He was closing his book.

"Yep, that too, I'm sure. He told us that he bought 'em because he truly believed they should be as common in this country as can openers."

"I imagine they are healthier than aspirins," Brook said, staring at her. He had this twinkle in his eye.

"Cheaper than psychiatrists," I added.

"More manageable than men," he said, watching me connect her.

"Fast as the speed of lightning," I said in the same tone as I threw back the covers, spread my legs, and switched her on.

I t was always difficult keeping Brook out of the kitchen. He loved to help me cook. This one particular evening "we" were preparing fresh pickerel, buttered brown rice, and spinach salad. Just as the fish started sizzling and about the time the Vouvray was properly chilled, he began to feel me out on a couple of thoughts that I imagine he'd had on his mind all day long. Much later on, too much later on, I wished I had told him the truth, not lied as I did.

"Are you sure you didn't mind Tommie coming by tonight?" he asked just as I started turning that fish. I kept my back turned so as not to have to look at him. I knew he was planning on watching my face for any negative signs.

"Nope, I didn't mind," I lied. "I like Tommie."

"Tell me if you minded," he said, "because whenever I've mixed my female friends together, I've seen troubled days. Women just can't seem to get along."

"Anyone that cares for you, I can care for, too," I lied as I clarified the butter in preparation for my special cannabis sauce. Brook enjoyed having a little weed with meals sometimes. "Someone loves you, I can love them," I said, turning off the burner and facing him for the first time since all of this began. "Understand?" He was holding his chin in his hands, staring down at the floor, not looking at me as I had assumed.

"In a way. Then you won't mind if I invite Pinkie over, too."

Pinkie? I thought, the hairdresser I'd just introduced him to less than six hours ago.

"I really like her. Do you?" he asked, lifting his chin from his hands, then pulling his fingers away from his fist with his other hand. This was a nervous habit of his. I turned back to the stove to check the rice.

The bitch, I thought as I slowly lifted the lid from the pot. I blushed as I recalled her asking me, "How does he do it?" "Very well," I'd quickly answered.

"Lewis," he said rather loudly, "you do like her, don't you?"

"She's pretty," I responded, stirring the rice with a

fork. I wanted to spit in it. "I like her. She's an awful lot like me. She's a Capricorn, too," I said, turning back around.

"Like you?" He couldn't hide his displeasure.

"Yeah," I said, lighting up a cigarette.

"Hmmm," he responded, pulling on his fingers.

"One time one of her husbands nearly stomped her to death in front of her house during a snowstorm. Seems like she called him a spineless pussy. Pinkie told me personally to only use those words long-distance. Those front teeth of hers are all new," I said, beginning to prepare his plate.

"Let's have a martini before dinner," he suggested as he backed himself out of the kitchen. "Put some of that stuff on our salad, too."

We ate our dinner mostly in silence. We had consumed a bottle of wine and a lot of "that stuff" before he began again.

"Is it normal for a woman to regularly masturbate?" he asked, scooping up a dose of salad. "Tommie said that the therapist believes it is quite natural. She prescribes one a day, sells vibrators right there in her office." What was he building up to this time? Maybe I never should have shown him Oh Baby.

"Let's open up that bottle of champagne in the refrigerator," he suggested as I walked toward the kitchen. "You ever used anything but Oh Baby?"

"Yep," I said, uncorking the champagne. "I tried a banana once. And a cucumber and a Polish sausage."

"Which did you prefer?" he asked, accepting a glass of the bubbly between his fists.

"The sausage, it was the most efficient. I was eliminating seeds for a week with the cucumber. Like a dummy I peeled it first. The banana crushed."

"If you'd had a few maraschino cherries and some ice cream, you could have had a banana split. Get it?" he asked, pounding his glass on the table for more champagne. His red eyes along with all this told me that he was zooming. "You ever used plain old fingers?"

"Never have," I lied.

"I wanna see you using plain old fingers," he said in a low, hoarse whisper, tossing his drink down.

"Right now?"

"Right now. Please," he said, looking me straight in my eyes with his mouth open.

You three?" was Brook's only comment after I finished telling him about how I would occasionally faint when Augus made love to me. K-K said I "swooned occasionally." "Puddin', your great big ol' blue eyes were partially open, just a respectable amount of saliva drooled out of the side of your pretty little lips. Looked like you had been shot with a blowgun." Here he threw himself onto his bed facedown, performing a few butterfly kicks, hysterically repeating "Blowgunner." "Augus said you were okay. He said it had happened before. I asked him if he would love me into nirvana, too. He said he'd try but I'd have to remain totally passive as you usually did. Too much activity could prevent that particular response."

"Rosemary tea soothes nerves. You oughta try a cup, Lewis." I didn't drink coffee or tea, seemed like I'd gone straight from mother's milk to alcohol. "Myth has it that when the Virgin was fleeing Herod with the Christ Child, she washed her blue cloak one night and hung it on a rosemary bush, whose flowers were white, to dry. The next morning the rosemary flowers had turned blue, and they have remained that way ever since. It's used as a charm against witches, too. And," Brook went on, "distributed at funerals to guard the dead, exchanged at weddings for luck." Go on, boy, I was thinking, pay me for my help in some more facts. They're usually more interesting than your advice. "Ancient Greek students drank it to clear their minds and refresh their memories. It has symbolized fidelity between lovers since the Romans," he rattled on. "You should send your playmates Augus and K-K a pound apiece," he suggested before he could stop this verbal rambling.

"Why?" I asked sweetly, placing his steaming mug of tea on his board slowly. He hated it when I caught him dragging his thick, silky veil of sophistication on the ground.

"To, ah, symbolize your fidelity," he responded, looking down into his tea.

"What is a pussy anyway but a slit with some hair on it, Kitty?" I asked on the telephone.

"That's what I have always said, Puddin'. What time is it out there, anyway? I've got my pretty little pink eyeshades on. Baby, Kitty partied last night. Princess and I discoed all over Midtown last night. One time I was out on the floor at Harrah's twitching around to the Trammps playing 'Seasons for Girls,' when suddenly I realized that I can't dance anymore."

"Can't dance?"

"Surely can't," he said in a Southern drawl, Scarlett O'Hara fashion. "Pretty Kitty is still twisting at the Peppermint Lounge with Chubby Checker, dahling. One time I think I dropped down into the early sixties.

I think I was doing The Pony. I was dancing out there on that glittery globe thing out of tune all by myself. Sure was good the kids were all stoned on amies and coke. I don't think anyone important noticed me ambling around. Princess had gone off with some sheik on his way to Saudi Arabia or something. She was convinced, it seems, that some of that oil money might leak on her. Forgive me, Angel, you called me to ask me something, didn't you? I'm sorry, Puddin'."

"You've already answered," I said, looking at myself in my bathroom mirror. Woody's stained-glass portrait of himself looking like a Buddha shaded the room just enough to make my face look tired instead of just plain puffy and old. "'Pussies are only slits with hair on them,'" I quoted. There's no reason for me to get hysterical because I found lipstick on Brook's collar and on his pillows.

"At least that's all they have ever been to me. But then you know what trouble I have convincing some of the fellas that what I've got for them is any better," he stated lazily.

"I don't see that what you've got is really any different," I said, looking for brown specks in my eyes. Prince had pointed out that the eyes age on a woman who drinks too much liquor. "The brown specks will finally dim those blues," he had said, dropping Murine into my eyes as he straddled me naked and long.

"Neither do I," Kitty said like Bette Davis. "I guess it's just where it's placed. I do have something, though," he said impishly, "that y'all don't have." I could see him stroking himself, lying there with his pink blinders on.

"What's that, K-K?" I asked, plucking some stray brow hairs.

"You know." I could see him lying there, rhythmically stroking himself. "What you got, too, pretty lady?" he cooed in a small boy's voice.

"A boy, I've got one, too. Brook discovered it for me." I could see Kitty picking up the rhythm of his strokes, imagining Brook finding mine.

"Thanks, Kitty," I said, quietly hanging up. "Peace and happiness await," I said to my lovely blue dolls that sat on my dresser.

As I sat waiting on Brook early one November morning in the corridor of this rehabilitation institute, I imagined humane nurses dressed in short, starched white uniforms sharing themselves with him. Wonder how many of these Florence Nightingales don't wear panties, I thought, watching three nurses wheel out a young blond football type strapped on his back to a table. I could see his urine draining into a plastic bag clamped to the side of his rolling table. They were all smiling at him. He was telling them about his accident. "This player tackled . . ." Another young man strapped facedown on a rolling table came pulling himself down the hall as they joyfully wheeled this hero onto the elevator. The door closed just as he reached it.

"Miss, will you push the Up button for me?" he asked, trying to hide his exasperation. "They didn't see me," he said. He wore his hair in cornrows, looked like an alley ballplayer.

"Sure will," I said, rising and heading for the elevator.

"What you writing?" he asked, looking up at my notebook and pencil that I clutched in my hand as I pushed the Up button.

"A list of stuff I have to do," I said as warmly as I could, hoping the elevator would come.

"See you," he said when the extra-wide doors opened. "Thanks." He pulled himself in as the attendant held the door.

I'd been writing this list while I waited for Brook to take his driving lesson. That way I hoped to avoid having to look at the Fellini-like character rolling by me.

1. Surgical supply house for new chair back (narrow)
2. Saks alteration department for pants
3. Gratiot Central Market
4. Bank
5. Kimbouroughs' Cleaners
6. Mrs. Richards's home
7. Main library

8. Weekend housekeeper—call to release her for weekend
9. Trim his beard and mustache
10. Drop boots at shoe shop for repair

This list was rather dull by comparison to other lists I had made in the days when I was high-stepping. Once my roommate Ciarra and I listed the names of each man we had ever fucked and remembered. We were sitting outside at a Greenwich Village restaurant, The Roadhouse, eating steamed clams, working on a third bottle of wine. The list was my idea. Then half an hour to analyze and categorize it. We were to put a check beside the once-onlys, a star beside the less-than-three-times, and a circle around the over-fives. After that we were to exchange lists and draw a line under the name of shared experiences.

Within an hour my list numbered eighty-eight. Ciarra's totaled two hundred exactly. She stopped when she couldn't remember any more names. Interpretation indicated that most of the "little experiences," as we labeled them, were one-timers. Cross-referencing confirmed our belief that we truly were sexually free. She blushed when she realized she'd listed Woody. Kitty, she said, grinning, was "the best." Just as we decided to write a list of

women, Ciarra spied an old "friend," as she called everyone. "Maybe this will be the day my friend waving over
there makes a star," she chirped. Without another word
she bounced across Seventh Avenue.

A smiling Brook appeared just as I was about to go
hide in the restroom from some more Fellini-like characters that were wheeling down the hall. I speculated as
his therapist pushed him toward me if I'd be there if he
were shorter, darker, kinky-haired.

Dr. Brook don't wanna know any characters like me outside of books, Lewis," Prince said first thing this one Saturday morning. "You shouldn't have sent me over there with those damned brownies." I'd gotten Prince to deliver a brown paper bag of brownies filled with nuts and weed the evening before. That's the only way Brook would take grass other than on a salad or in spaghetti sauce. I would have taken them myself had it not been Friday. Friday was not "my" day; Friday was Tommie's day.

"This lady let me in on her way out. She had the reddest lips and most pointed tits I've ever seen."

"Mrs. Richards, the housekeeper," I volunteered. I wondered if Tommie had run and hid in his office the

way she usually did if he had a surprise visitor. Brook
swore he didn't find anything off about that habit; as
a matter of fact, he liked her shyness, he said, found it
feminine.

"No, I didn't give her the cookies, my dear. It took
him almost five minutes to roll himself out of his bedroom into his living room. His battery was dead on his
electric one. I didn't think he was ever gonna make it.

"When he first saw me standing there browsing
through one of his books, he immediately put his dukes
up. I musta looked just like unadulterated Native Son
to him. First thing he did after we shook hands was to
throw that wooden board from where he was parked to
the couch. Bam!" Prince clapped his hands to imitate the
sound of Brook's board as it hit. "Then he kicked first his
right foot pedal aside, then his left foot pedal, dropping
both of his feet to the ground. Thud! Thud! I started to
throw those damned cookies at him and run before he
got up and walked. I felt his power. Yes sirree bob, I did.
He sat so rigid in that chair that I started to salute him
and leave quickly."

"What stopped you?"

"His eyes, baby. He caught me with those big blues
of his. I was really all his when he started talking to me,
looking up at me. It must be a bitch to be a man of his
size and have to look up at sons of bitches all the time,"

Prince said, softly kissing me good morning on the nape of my neck. "He invited me to stay for lunch. He'd made this seafood salad with me in mind. Until I saw that he couldn't get the bowl out of the refrigerator, I thought he had actually made it. Without you, Lewis, me and Brook and me and Woody could be friends," Prince said as he pulled the covers off me. His tongue felt dry and hot as he traveled down my back with it slowly. "I bet Dr. Brook loved your ass, too, boy. He has strong-looking jawbones."

"He's perfect from the neck up." Prince climbed upon my back as we talked.

"Let me in, Lewis," Prince demanded. "I'm coming through the back, girl." Gracefully he pushed this door open and slowly entered. I'd gotten Kitty to show me how to relax. He'd sworn afterward that I gave him as much pleasure as any of the guys. The problem we faced was one of reciprocation. "What you thinking about, babe?" Prince asked, noticing my silence.

"Thinking about Kitty-Kat," I responded. "What you thinking?" I hoped he'd be careful like Kitty.

"I was thinking about Brook," he replied, increasing the beat. "This one is for Brook, Lewis," he squealed as he emptied himself within me.

C an't keep a secret, can you? Can you? I thought as I checked the glass in the sink. I'd cleared that sink right before I'd left the night before.

"Morning, Lewis," Brook squeezed out groggily with his eyes closed. "Enjoy your movie with Woody?" I was now standing at his bedroom door, stretching my lips.

"We didn't go. I was too tired. Enjoy yours? How's Tommie?"

"Don't know. I haven't spoken to her in a week or so." He looked up at me innocently as I yanked his empty urinal from between his thighs. "I haven't had to void since you left," he added, watching me lift his covers in order to replace the urinal between his legs. Glancing at his feet, I noted that his socks were off, too. I'd left them on purposefully.

"How long did it take you to get out of your socks by yourself?" I asked, lowering the covers.

"Quite a while," he said calmly, beginning to waken fully now.

"Lewis," he called out, trying to stop me.

"And that lipstick on your shirt collar couldn't possibly be mine. I never get an opportunity to put it on anymore. We haven't even hugged this week." I was building. "Why do you have to lie to me? 'A quiet evening alone' was what you requested. You were afraid my help was taking your independence away. Just a little 'privacy to think.'" I was building and crying now, standing at the foot of his bed.

"Okay! An old friend called and stopped by last night. She helped me to bed. She used to help me," he explained.

"An old friend named Tommie," I said, picking her pink terry cloth slippers up from the foot of the bed. "I left these at the head of your bed where anyone wanting them would have to look for them and know they're there in the first place." With this I threw her slippers up on his chest. "Why? Why don't you want me to know when you see her? I want you to have friends—women friends. I honestly do."

"You just want to have the right of approval. You just

want the right of control. You just want too much in return for your assistance!" he screamed out at me.

"You are mostly correct, I guess," I said, letting our
eyes hold each other for a few seconds. "Cooperation cuts
down on conflict. Sneaking is not necessary. And it is an
antiquated custom."

"For you, maybe! Discretion, privacy, mean sneaking
to you. You make beautiful words sound like nasty hab-
its. How do you do it?"

"By thinking a lot," I responded quickly. "I think a
lot. Right now I think, since it is early Saturday morning
and we are both still tired, that I should just go into the
living room and lie down," I said, walking past his bed.

"I haven't been able to stop you from doing whatever
you want thus far. Go ahead. Do whatever pleases you,"
he said.

Lying on his couch, I cried out of weariness. I prayed,
too.

One morning we couldn't get it up long enough to put it into the rubber urinal. After a most exasperating hour of quietly waiting on him to have a psychic erection, I boldly asked if I could give it a try.

"That won't help," he said, flushing pink.

"Relax and let me," I said, bending down for it.

"Do as you like," he said, closing his eyes with a sigh.

"You've gotta watch," I said.

"You look at him, too, dummeee!" Sestra said. "Remember what I told you about Brook's eyes."

We looked at each other as I cajoled it with my tongue.

"There are some things you do not know about me, Lewis," he said, closing his eyes.

"Ignore him!" Sestra commanded.

"Get on top of me," he said. "Keep me warm and he might come on out." I felt slightly like a sow sitting on a crate of eggs. "Press your nipples," he began, "into mine, hard, hug me," he said with his eyes closed. "That's good. Give me your nose. Now take mine, Lewis," he instructed quietly. "That's it," he said slowly. "Oh yes! Oh yes!" The long hairs that covered his legs became moist with my secretions as I burrowed into him. Connecting.

Brook, don't depend upon me being a lady much longer," I said, helping him slide into my car.

"Depend upon your being a lady?" he asked, emphasis on "your." "Can't depend upon something that isn't," he said, sliding into Woody's beige upholstery.

"Why did you have to pick her to court?" I asked, pushing his long legs into my car. "She's not rich, not good-looking."

"She is very talented," he commented as I hooked my safety belt around his body. "She writes music. She is a copywriter for a big ad company, twenty-five thousand a year base salary. When have you last earned a salary, Lewis?" he asked as I pulled him into a leaning position. "I like her voice. It's resonant, soothing to my ear."

"Can she drive a car?" I casually asked before I slammed the car door shut.

"Of course, she has a new Stingray," he proudly responded.

"Has she got a telephone?" I asked.

"I guess," he said quietly, beginning to catch the drift I was on.

"Well, Dr. Brook, may I suggest that you get out of this old Cadillac and call her to come get you to take you to the rehabilitation institute in her new Stingray. I have decided that I have something better to do." With that I took his chair and began pushing it back to the building. That chair looked like a riderless horse.

Tommie must have left when I rang the buzzer to indicate I was on my way up. Her slippers were sitting in the hallway, still warm. Gingerly, just as I would two lumps of shit, I picked them up by their heels, marched them into his bathroom. He must have felt me holding them over his toilet wastebasket. "No one bothers *your* things," he said from his bedroom. He had watched me coming down the hallway with them in this mirror he had set up for that purpose.

"What things? I don't have anything over here but a toothbrush." With this I dropped her slippers into that basket. They needed washing anyway, I thought, walking into his bedroom and over to his window. There she was, scraping the snow off her car. She looked like she should have on a pink snowsuit. I bet she sat on the fire exit steps and waited until she was sure I was inside. One day I planned to buzz him, then rush wildly to those back stairs and catch her as she ran down them. How're you doing, Miss Gunn? I'd say, smiling sweetly as we passed each other on the steps. How's our favorite man feeling today, Miss Gunn? Did you turn him over on his side before you left? Or do I have to do it, Miss Gunn?

"I put your little friend's scuffs in the trash. They need washing," I said, still watching her out the window.

"No, they don't. They're none of your business, Lewis." He was turned on his side. "My friend doesn't use your scented soap. Nor does she use your cute little crocheted French shopping bags. There is no contest in this house. Can't you understand that? Tommie stayed over last night because it was late and her car wouldn't start. She did a lot of typing for me."

"What can I do for you?" I asked, watching her back her car up out of his assigned space. I had to park in the public lot.

"You can empty this can for me. It's full. She respects you, Lewis," he said as I removed the steel urinal from between his legs. It smelled strong this morning. I'd have to be sure to give him his bladder pills. "She doesn't perceive of me as a territory. I'm her friend. We help each other. We respect each other."

"You lie a lot," I said. "I'm tired of sharing. Do you wanna lie on your back now?" I asked, pulling away the pillows that braced him before he could respond.

"No! Be my friend," he pleaded as I prepared to turn him onto his back.

"Nope."

"Friendship's what I have to give, Lewis."

"Friend? Sister? Either title means that I don't get fucked. Woody thinks I'm his sister. I asked him the other night as we lay in his bed to do more than hug me. He said that would be like incest to him."

"Does it matter what we call each other?"

"Probably doesn't."

"So?" He sounded cheerful now that this was all over. Settled.

"So? Call me 'My Woman.' I like that. Or can you think of something more appropriate?"

"How about 'Bitch'?" he said, chuckling.

"How about 'The Bitch' for distinction?"

"A Bitch," he offered quickly, beaming.

"I've got it," I said, slowly sitting down on the edge of his bed, placing my arms around his body.

"Okay! Shoot!" he said, accepting a small kiss.

"How about 'My Bitch'?" I asked.

G reat-grandmama got sick, my Auntie Hessie said, 'cause they didn't let her have a man," Sestra told me one morning over coffee. "I know now what she was going through, Lewis. Sometimes I accidentally touch myself as I bathe and can't stop until I get it out. Waking alone in the middle of the night throbbing is the worst. No man. Sometimes I wanna throw back my covers, open up the windows, and cry out for any man I've ever known to relieve myself. My nipples ache the most," she added, lighting up an extra-long low-tar cigarette. She was a two-pack-a-day lady. Often I've wondered how she kept her breath smelling so sweet. Sometime I'm gonna ask her how she does it. Momentarily I fought the desire to touch her long, fleshy lips. Sestra worked her lips like some say girls should work their twats—slowly and methodically opening and closing them on that cigarette. "I'd get one of those vibrators you're always promoting, but they're too noisy." She gave me lots of eyes as she caressed her cigarette with her lips. Then she continued, "The sound might wake up my kids." I tried to decide whether I should unveil myself more to her and tell about the new transistorized ones. Crushing out her cigarette, she studied me as I watched the uncrossing of her three and one half feet of naked legs. Solidly planting her size eleven feet upon a velvet dining chair, she reached for another long brown cigarette. "My heat is showing up in my stomach nowadays. Great-grandmama, Auntie said, used to throw up at night, too. I bet she just needed to be touched all over. Probably wondered as I do why she believed that a good woman should keep her mind and her honey box separate all of the time."

"'Cause bad girls get babies," I interrupted. "'Cause bad girls hurt their mamas."

"'Cause bad girls are free," she chanted back.

"'Cause the 'mens' won't want you anymore," I added.

"You can stifle the desire for a long time," Sestra continued, "but it surfaces at just about the time your youthfulness leaves. Our breasts begin to sag as our bellies dry up and our asses slacken. That entrapped hot liquid thickens with age." Calmly, she examined one of her legs for varicose veins. "It feels heavy all locked inside, Lewis."

"No one you can trust to give it to becomes no one you want wants any," I whispered. Sestra kept her eyes fastened on another butt, which she slowly ground into a clear, cut-glass crystal ashtray. "That's about the time they start calling a woman 'my friend.' Men, I think, believe vintage pussy comes dry like vintage champagne."

"Great-grandmama hurt," Sestra repeated, getting up and walking into her kitchen for more black coffee. She wore one of those long nylon gowns. It was the kind that women get in pastels or white from their kids and in red or black from their men. Hers were always too short to cover all of her. She walked back slowly, as if she felt weighty. Sestra was big, not fat. "By the time you really need a man," she said, lifting her coffee cup, "they don't need you. As our lust increases, our opportunities decrease. Ain't that the truth? Doesn't seem fair to use your wisdom to seduce young boys."

"We don't usually even consider them. And don't look at girls, either. 'Once one of them awful mannish things touches you, you become one of them,'" I blurted out, smiling at the memory of that myth.

"Dimmed eyes, lost dreams, sagging ass, loose stomach, thickening veins, sour breath," I chanted, sinking into her doleful brown eyes. I wondered as we melted into each other's eyes why we listened to our mamas. I saw all those ceilings I had stoically stared at as I submitted to one or another of them. I wished I'd reached out more. "Brook claims I am such a bitch in the morning."

"He doesn't know why?"

"He says he really doesn't."

"He knows," she responded, looking down at her crystal ashtray full of stale butts.

Sometimes Brook would get nasty as I undressed him. Usually I ignored him, ever since Woody asked me to imagine what it must feel like not to sit up without help. This one morning, however, I forgot Woody's words. Probably because he'd awakened me every hour, it seemed, to turn him over. He "thought" he felt pressure building up on his skin. Prolonged pressure would break down his skin, causing sores to develop. I became as frightened of this occurring as he was.

"I remind you of the Gerber baby, don't I?" he asked as I began to put on his pants.

"A bit," I responded.

"You enjoy many aspects of my state. I know you do."

"Like what?" I was slipping on his socks.

"Like controlling. Like the fact that my nasty ol' sperm can't hurt you." As I zipped up his boots: "Like I can't kick your ass." He smiled at this as I pulled him into a sitting position. We remained silent as I placed his board under his hips and onto his chair. One mistake on my part and he could land on the floor. As I held his ankles to help propel him into his chair by a series of co-ordinated pushes, he went on, "I'm right about you. You know I am." I remained silent as I placed his feet upon his foot pedals, pulled his pants out of his crotch, and placed the right arm on the chair.

"So what if you are right?" I asked, placing his board across his armrests. "Aren't you just lucky to know me, then? What could you do with a woman that needed a sperm-thrusting ass kicker?" He remained silent as I pulled his chair out of his bedroom and into his bathroom so that he could brush his teeth in front of the mirror.

"You are the most arrogant, bullheaded, aggressive person I have ever known. You are a bully." He was fighting to find more release. His frustration showed in the way he tightly held on to his wooden board. I just knew that he wanted to sling it. "First you take over my house—"

"By your invitation," I spat back.

"Then you chase away my friend." His eyes were rimmed in red, drippy-looking.

"Good friends can't be chased away by me," I retorted.

"You involve her parents in our business."

"Shouldn't fool around with dependents," I slammed back.

"You are an embarrassment to me. Humiliation means nothing to you."

"Not the kind you are speaking of," I said, lighting a cigarette.

"Get out of my life. Leave me alone. I have no passion for you. Don't you see that?"

"You have a need. I know that for sure. Who taught you that passion is a prerequisite for survival, anyway?"

"I do not love you, woman," he shot out now with the first tears.

"There you go, using those schoolboy words again," I said, shaking my finger at him teacher-like. "I don't think you understand that pompous words mean nothing to me."

"One of the bizarre things about you is that you have decided to manipulate words to suit you."

"And why not, creep?" I was getting angry now. I felt my eyes bulging out of control. "Jesus, Gandhi, Hitler, Churchill, Martin Luther King, Jr., did. Why not Lewis? Words have no life without interpretation." My armpits were wet, letting off that ancient smell.

"Interpretation. You want interpretation?" he managed to get out of his distorted face. "Here is interpretation—catch," he commanded. With all of the power his living muscles could muster he slung that wooden board.

I screamed as it landed in my chest. All I could do was stand there. Next he kicked his foot pedals back. Then he dropped first one foot and then the other.

"If I could reach you, I would plant this Bally boot solidly up your fat ass."

Before I could stop myself, I dashed up near him. Then I turned my back to him and stooped over, tooting my behind up to him. "You wanna farm, creep?" I dared. "Farm," I directed. "Plant it right here." As I said this, I looked back. At just this instant he was lifting his right leg with his arms. That Bally boot landed right in my face, knocking me off balance, knocking him off balance. We hit the floor, me first.

"Oh, baby," he yelled. "I'm sorry. I'm sorry. Are you

hurt? Did I hurt you?" Bunches of tears were shooting out of us, hot ones.

I lay silently on that old green carpet, holding the right side of my face. Painstakingly he began to crawl over to me by using my body as a pull. He looked like an eel, folding and then unfolding.

"Oh my God, Lewis. Why? Why do you do this to us?" he murmured as he crawled. "Lewis, you have no competition. There is no contest between us. For Christ's sake, baby, why are you at war always?"

"Guess I've never known peace," I said as he finally pulled himself up beside me. "I was brought up on conflict, misery, hostility. My mothers passed it down. My daddies didn't stick around long enough to stop them," I mumbled out. Tears, snot, and spit were running out of both of us now. We were holding on to each other.

"Didn't know enough to stop them, Lewis. Your daddies, perhaps, did not know how to stop them. Boys hurt, too, you know that? They don't all have peace."

"Skin's not broken," he whispered through tears as he examined my face. He lifted his hand and dropped it softly on my bruised face. "Don't know my own strength, I guess. First time I ever hit a woman."

"All the fellas say that," I joked. Brook massaged my face with his lips and his eyes now. "I don't want to love you, Brook. I don't want to love any man. It's like I've been assigned to love you. I wasn't expecting you. I was all ready to take up needlepointing or something."

Talking like this, we held each other until the ache subsided.

Any New Yorker can tell you that a New Yorker's senses are really dulled when he steps into a pile of dog shit. That's what I did as I skidded off the curb at LaGuardia with Brook. He'd have been tossed out onto the pavement had Kitty not been there.

"Buckle up for safety, Brook. There's a bumpy road ahead," Kitty quoted, holding on to Brook. "Welcome to New York City, dahling."

"This is my first time," Brook confided, looking a bit uncomfortable when Kitty pushed him up to this rented stretch limousine.

"I wanted to introduce you the way I was introduced."

"How's that?" Brook asked.

"By a chauffeur-driven limo. I was sixteen, traveling

with this richie-poo," he explained, handing Brook's briefcase to the driver. "This is Martin. There she is, Buster," Kitty said, pointing toward Manhattan.

"I've studied the Manhattan street maps so long, I feel I've been here before," Brook said, accepting his glass. "I'd like to see Fifth Avenue first."

"Not Harlem?" Kitty asked, beaming.

"Perhaps on our way back," Brook responded. "I've seen quite enough of it in the movies. To me, driving through Harlem would be the same as touring Auschwitz before the survivors were removed."

"Martin, take us down Fifth Avenue first," Kitty instructed softly through the partition.

I began to relax with my third glass of bubbly. To forget about missing two planes the day before because Brook would allow no one to drive him to the airport but Tommie Gunn. And she got lost twice. As we neared 100th and Fifth my stomach muscles tightened. I'd spent three months in Mt. Sinai's psychiatric section the last time I was in town. I stared at the building as we passed, trying not to relive the scene that had tripped me. I'd been out on the town with Augus and Kitty. We'd started with dinner at La Trattoria de Alfredo on Bank Street. Then Reno Sweeney's for Novella Nelson's show. We loved Novella Nelson passionately at the time.

We'd blown all our cocaine by the time Kitty

suggested we go to this party over on Sutton Place. He guaranteed us the queen that was throwing it would have lots of drugs. We dropped the acid and our clothes at the door. Then we were escorted into this huge bedroom where the party was in full force. There was a blazing fireplace, about a dozen people, and this incredible bed that sat three feet off the floor. Perched dead center surrounded by half a dozen bodies was our host, who was wearing a brass mask. The most interesting people, however, were not on the bed. They were the three tuxedoed musicians over in the corner: violin, bass, and flute. They smiled the same way I imagined they'd smile if they were playing for a wedding.

Kitty immediately pushed me up on that bed. Before I could greet our host, a hand reached out and squeezed my left breast. I remember watching Kitty kissing our host through the hole in his mask. And holding on to Augus as he covered me with his body to keep anyone else from touching me. And the fear I felt when that dark music-filled room became all colors to me.

When I started screaming and exactly how Kitty and Augus got me into that hospital, I don't remember. They say I tried frantically to pull off that queen's mask before he threw us off his set.

"So this is Rockefeller Center?" Brook touched my

hand, bringing me back. Martin turned onto Rockefeller Plaza, parked in back of another identical limousine, cut the motor, and got out. I sensed that I had missed something along the way.

"Kitty says there is nothing more exciting than sitting on this street, watching the herds of people march by, eating Sabrett, and drinking all the Yoo-hoos you want," Brook explained as Martin returned with the lunch.

"Kitty-Kat suggested that I sleep on the sofa bed tonight," I whispered to Brook. I was helping him slide from his chair onto Kitty's bed. "Claims he has acquired a backache from sleeping on that thing."

"Tell you what. I'll sleep on the sofa. Let go of my feet and come grab my shoulders. I wanna stay in my chair." Before he could finish, I shoved his feet forward and he was pitched into bed. I moved forward, throwing myself onto him, holding until his spasms subsided. I loved to feel the vibrations they created. I'd pretend he was shaking out of passion. Just as I got into his neck, he started tossing his head from side to side. This was his way of moving out of my way.

"I appreciate Kitty's hospitality. He is a fine chap.

And he isn't the first of his kind that I have known. Hospitals are staffed by lots of gay nurses. Several of my helpers are."

"But none of your friends."

"Not to my knowledge. I'm not a prick, Lewis. I don't care about a person's sexual preferences. I'm simply exhausted by the drama you two create. Together you're not people. You're actors. Always on stage. I don't want to be on stage. I'm a very private person. I like obscurity."

Brook swore that without his chair he was basically your average scholarly type. I was unlocking his red suspenders when he got to the point. "Augus has made us a reservation at the Algonquin Hotel for the rest of our stay. He says a man of letters like myself belongs there."

"Is Gussy paying, too?" I had noticed the 30 percent tip he'd left at the Coach House earlier that evening. "He's so generous with our money."

"We're not paying. I am." The flow of his speech was interrupted by his voiding. "I want you to get some rest. Kitty agrees. He's gonna take you and our bags down there tomorrow while I meet Hillary at the University Club for lunch."

Slowly I undressed him, resenting all of them for daring to make decisions without me. I was exhausted. Brook had forced more of New York City into a week than I'd seen in a year. As I emptied his rubber urinal into the toilet, he screamed out for me. Before he said my name twice, I was back in that room. I remembered that time his chair had tipped over when he reached down to try to pick up a book on the floor. And that time he'd almost choked on a chocolate. There he was, lying there on Kitty's bed, wearing only a green T-shirt and a pair of argyle socks, laughing, looking down between his legs. And there it was, standing straight up. I'd forgotten that his looked like the one everybody wanted.

"Make this disappear," he suggested.

"How?" I asked.

"Sit on it! Hurry, Lewis! This is a miracle. Easy, Lewis," he pleaded as I lifted my slip and slowly slid down on it. "That's it," he kept saying as I worked it. "What's it feel like to you? Tell! Does it feel dead?"

"It feels like mine." With this I reared back, placing my ankles over his shoulders. "Let him see!" Sestra shouted within me. *Feel like making love* ran through my head. "Feel like making love?" I asked, looking at the stars that danced upon his ceiling.

"Feel like making love," he sighed.

"The next time Brook sees you," K-K said breathlessly, "I want you looking fresh. Take a hot bubble bathette and put this on." He unzipped my garment bag and whipped out the black silk dress.

"You bought that for me, Kitty?"

"No, ac-tu-al-ly, I bought it for myself. I was gonna go cruising in drag. But when it came time to shave off my mustache, I couldn't do it." I broke and started weeping. "Highlight those baby blues with extra makeup tonight," he instructed, wiping my tears away. "When we get back here, I'll call you to come down. Take fifteen minutes after to rest. Then meet us in the Rose Room. Order a bottle of champagne for the suite, an expensive bottle, Puddin'."

"You look tired, K-K," I said, kissing that beautiful man's eyelids. "Brook is moving around on both of our energies."

"I can look tired. I'm a man," he whispered. "Weariness makes a man seem hard-working, serious about life. It gives character to him and his face. It makes a woman look like a stale loaf of unpreserved bread instead of a fresh cookie."

"See those people over there?" I whispered as the tuxedoed waiter pushed Brook's chair expertly up to the table.

"Lewis, why must you speak so loudly? Whoever it is is surely not deaf like you think I am," he said, opening up the menu.

"Welcome to the Oyster Bar, sir. Cocktails before dinner?"

"May we see the wine list?" Brook politely asked.

"Certainly, sir!"

"I'd like a dry vodka first. Their bartenders make the finest martinis in New York," I said, still whispering.

"All I need this evening is for Kitty to arrive and find you drinking. He'll start drinking, too. Before ten o'clock he will have turned into a punk and you'll be red-eyed, foul-mouthed, and drunk. Please, Lewis, try it my way tonight."

"Okay! Only because you're so pretty and—"

"Because I'm so right. You know it. I want you sober. I can't stop Kitty. He's not my friend, as you are. He's your friend."

"Speak of the Pumpkin, there he is," I said as Kitty entered the room. He entered as if he were expected by everyone. Kitty was beautiful in a creamy beige suit with a dark brown shirt and white silk tie. His skin glowed in those lights.

"Why is he going over to those people?" Brook whispered.

"He knows them. They're the people I was trying to tell you about earlier," I said, picking up my napkin and placing it on my lap. The Plaza's napkins were so well starched they looked like paper. "Remember I told you about my neighbors? The rich freaks I told you about? That's them. That couple they're with are the owners of that swing farm in New Jersey."

"Why didn't you speak to each other?" he asked quietly as he accepted the wine list from the waiter. The man has such style, I thought as I watched Brook study that list.

Kitty was moving slowly around that table now, passing out kisses, cheeks for the women, lips for the men. He loved threatening freaks in public. "The fat cat watches his wife frolic in the hay with other women. Stands and jerks off for a few of his select friends while he watches. I saw him come so hard one time, it looked like he'd turned on a fire hose. I'm hungry. Kitty is going to keep playing with those creeps for a while."

Noticing the waiter was taking our order, Kitty swished over. "You smell even better than you look, man," Brook said. Men always liked to remind Kitty that he was a man.

"I'm wearing Tabu," he said, bending over and taking a kiss from Brook before Brook could duck.

"How you doing, ba-bee?" he said, coming around to greet me.

"I was doing fine until you started your slut act over there. Why did you go over there? If I could have quietly changed us to the Oak Room, I would've. I don't like being in the same city with them. You know that."

"Oh, ba-bee, I think they're cute. Just 'cause Lewis got bored up at the farm and caused one of her grand drunken scenes, Brookie," he said, giving Brook lots of eyes, "she wants Kitty to give up the farm, too. Never, baby, it's free, the food's great, the music is out of this world, and the guests are fabulous. Nothing barred except poor manners. That's why Lewis is barred," he said, smiling in that cherubic style of his as he daintily spread his napkin. "Did you order my martini, Angel?" he asked, looking at Brook.

"No, but I will. Sir," Brook said softly to our passing waiter. "A Stolichnaya martini straight up with a lemon twist for my guest. Rocks on the side. We're having wine with our dinner," he said, looking at me. "Lewis is under the impression that they are threatened by her promise to expose them," Brook said, indicating to the waiter that his appetizer of crepes was to be placed by me. His nod toward me indicated that it was all right if I cut it up for him.

"Oh, my dear, they are afraid of our little girl's exposure. See, those lovely couples are closet freaks. To see them at church, you would never know how they get down at that farm."

"I think they're hypocrites. They live a lie," I said, easing a bit of crepe into my mouth.

"But, baby, they live so very well. They know who they are. They don't have to advertise it the way some of us do," he said, making a funny face at me.

"I just couldn't get into them. Kitty had a ball."

"Or two," K-K added. "Me lady here wants relationships. We," he said, looking toward the other couples, "simply want to have fun."

"What do you want for dinner, Kitty?" Brook asked, beckoning the waiter.

"A triple martini on the rocks, an olive, and a smile from our girl," he said, reaching across the table to touch my face.

touched him on his elbow to indicate that I planned to counter his hold. It was a dangerous one we were in at that point," he said, staring out of his eyes that were focused on twenty years ago. "It's been outlawed now in wrestling. He threw me over his head," Brook said. "He didn't let go of my neck as he threw me." His eyes were leading me into his past. "I heard my neck snap," he said, grimacing. "There were bright lights and screaming. I was thrashing around like a chicken on that floor, I guess. The screams were my mother's," he stated, focusing back on me. I'd waited six months for him to tell me how his neck was broken. We were sitting in the sculpture garden at the Museum of Modern Art when I'd finally asked him about that night.

"My mother had stopped at my school to pick me up for Christmas vacation. We were going to a friend's home on Martha's Vineyard. My dad was to fly up from Nashville, join us." Dilated pupils relayed his mother screaming as she ran from her seat onto that floor. Knowing Brook as I did by this time, I was thinking Brook probably had insulted that big blond boy in some way. Sestra had told me that personally she thought Brook was an evil son of a bitch—pre-accident. She said he'd told her that his father sent him away out east to school because his father thought he'd end up in prison if he didn't get him out of Nashville. Brook had told her that he kept a bayonet under his bed at school just in case the other boys got rough with him.

"My opponent at some point jumped on top of me, pinned me down. The coach, I'm told, pulled him off me. When I awakened, I was in the hospital, strapped down from my head to my ankles. My mother was standing over me, crying. All I could move was my eyeballs. She told me I had pinched a nerve. That's what she was telling herself." He blinked himself back into that garden at this realization, smiled faintly.

"What is it?" I asked.

"I was thinking about the night before that 'fateful evening,' as Mother used to call it. I had a date with this beautiful young girl from the girls' school down the road.

Oasis, my first lover. I was her first, too. We slipped into this boarded-up farmhouse, cuddled and cooed as long as we could," he said, smiling at me. "I still remember how it felt inside of her. I didn't want to come out. She smelled like ripe cantaloupe and fresh strawberries." Surprised by his confession, he looked out into the museum's garden as a slight spasm eased through his body. "I married her five years later!" he reported, turning back to me. "She left me a note one day when I was a senior at Vanderbilt. You'll like this part, Lewis," he added, "you're such a romantic. The note said she really did care, but she had to love herself for a while, had to rest. She said I was Dracula." I fought a loud hoot at this. "I never saw her again. She sent me a picture of herself and her three tow-headed children from Sweden ten years later. The note on the back of the picture simply said, 'Forgive me.'"

"Hey, Dracula," I said loudly enough to startle him out of that reverie. "Pablo Picasso's *Guernica* is somewhere in this joint. Wanna explain the *Guernica* to me?"

"Sure do," he responded, forcing the tears back inside.

The fourth and last morning we spent at his apartment, Kitty playfully sneaked into the guest bedroom. I had just helped Brook turn over. As I was about to turn so that I might bury my face in Brook's wonderful neck, Kitty sprang up off the floor where he'd crawled from the door.

"Woman!" he yelled as he leaped into bed on top of me. "I want it! I've heard so much about it," he said, mimicking Orson Welles. With this, Kitty proceeded to try to pull the covers back. I held on tightly.

"What's going on, K-K?" Brook asked softly. I'm sure he was holding on to his covers too, by now.

"I've heard, man, that this hussy here has some of the best stuff in town. And I want some," he said, winking at me, rubbing his nose on mine. "Let's take her against her will," he suggested.

"I'm always taken that way, creep," I blurted out, giving him a kiss. Brook was trying to look over his shoulder to see what we were doing. Kitty was grinding away on top of me. I was laughing hysterically.

"What you're going to get, Kurt, is hot urine all over us and your fancy bed. You and Lewis want to play," he said, trying to hide his irritation, "then help me to get up, please. Or get out of the bed and go somewhere else. You're like having two children around all the time. There is more to life than playing," he said, beginning to uncomfortably void loudly at this time.

"Like what, may I ask?" Kitty responded in Eartha Kitt's voice. "Like what? Discipline? Debts? Distress? Disillusionment? Dishonesty? Deceit?" Before Brook could respond, K-K nimbly jumped off me, toe-danced around his bed, yanked the covers off Brook, grabbed his warm urinal, and asked in his own voice, "Like dis?" peering into that urinal. Thrusting those covers back on an embarrassed Brook, K-K threw his gorgeous head back, turned, and began to make his exit as a majorette would do. At the door, in Lena Horne's voice, he continued, "Buster, I just came in here to get the can, to empty it. Next time I'm sitting on the toilet pee-peeing I won't think about dem," he said, pointing toward

Brook's genitals. With that, out he swished, slamming the door.

Brook's old schoolmate Hillary was conservative from his wing-tipped shoes to his blue oxford cloth shirt. And he spoke seven languages! The three of us were sitting around one of those little tables with the bells, sipping white wine, chatting eloquently on elegant topics. Hillary was comparing the voice of Grace Bumbry to Leontyne's when Kitty appeared. He was wearing a winter-white suit that was completely drenched. From the way he glided toward us, I knew he was soused. Brook was the only one who did not see him or he certainly would have ducked the kiss that K-K planted on his cheek.

"What you doing, K-K? Playing hide-and-seek?"

"Nope," K-K replied drunkenly, "but I sure would like to with your friend over there." Then he just stood there, weaving, waiting.

"I'm Hillary Helms," Hillary said, extending a well-manicured hand to Kitty. "How are you, man?"

"Just a little damp, man," Kitty responded. "Order me a drink, honey," he said to Brook, "while I find myself a chair."

"Do you want another drink, Lewis?" Brook asked me.

"Triple bourbon and branch water, honey," I said to

Brook. Before I could smile, Hillary daintily tapped the bell on our table.

"Isn't that quaint," Kitty said as he forced his chair between Brook and Hillary. "At first I thought I was so drunk I was hearing things. I just love all this," he said, pointing at the room. "Never imagined I'd be sitting here ringing for service. Everybody here is probably wondering who we are, I betcha. In case you're wondering, I got drenched cruising down Broadway. I met this beautiful Brazilian. He's gonna meet me later at Harrah's. Y'all wanna come?"

"I'm afraid I can't," Hillary said, impatiently hitting that bell.

"Try clapping, man. Maybe the poor waiter's tone-deaf from all the ringing. Order me a triple bourbon and branch water, man."

"Two triple bourbons and bottled water," Hillary said the moment our waiter appeared. "And two more glasses of Riesling Mosel."

All of them looked like Kitty to me as they passed by looking at me in my cage. Kitty kept saying, "You were a bad girl, baby. You forgot your manners again, Puddin'. We were having so much fun until then. Angel, you were very un-la-dy-like. You really let go this time. Oh, love,

I was just trying to shut you up. Brook tried in his own eloquent style. That man is really flawless. You, my dear, were a brute. You wouldn't let go of his chair so that Hillary could take him to the University Club for dinner. You screamed right out in clear Anglo-Saxon in the middle of the Algonquin lobby at Brook. 'Bitch,' you said. 'Bitch, you are not leaving me tonight. You are staying right here with me!' Ba-bee, that posh crowd tried not to stare. They kept talking louder to each other, trying not to see you holding on to that poor defenseless man. Brook does look defenseless to strangers, you know that. Then, when you couldn't get Brook to stay with you, you started on us. Me, your loving Kitty-Kat, became 'you punk mother-fucker son of a bitch.' Then you spit on Hillary. That's when I grabbed you and pulled you out of that lobby into a cab. I think he was going to fight you like the man you were talking and acting like."

"Why, Kitty?" I asked one of them that looked like Kitty. "Why?"

"You kept mumbling that you were tired of sharing. I brought you first to my apartment. Before we got through the door, you puked and blacked out on the floor.

"Puddin', I tried to get Brook not to leave you here. He said that he couldn't take any more. Hillary found your Valium in the bathroom cabinet as he packed

Brook. Brook said he had almost adjusted to the liquor and cigarettes, couldn't take the pills, too.

"Baby doll, people like him prefer characters like us in books or on stages. We got off our track, Angel Face. This is East Coast, Ivy League, blue blood."

"Where am I, Kitty?" I asked, recognizing Kitty.

"You're in a hospital. I left you alone at the apartment to go back to the hotel to check on Brook. Guess you wakened, thought I'd deserted you, too. You, my dear, tried to hang yourself from my track lights. Fortunately, you'd gained all that weight. You pulled them out of the ceiling. I called Woody. Woody told me to call an ambulance and bring you here. The only thing wrong with you now is a sore throat and a hangover." He laughed at his little pun.

"Does Brook know I'm here?" I asked.

"He does. He said he'd call you. To let him call you. Such a gentleman, isn't he, baby?"

Brook hadn't had a shower or bath in four years when I met him. He'd only been "sponged off" in bed. I managed to change this a little for him. Gradually I sneaked in perfumed pink bubbles, a pink nail brush, and a pink Japanese scrub cloth. I dreamed about the day I could bathe him in the Atlantic right after he freely took a piss in the white sand. He said he'd compromise with me and make an appointment to be given a bath at rehab.

Usually he watched the news shows as I scrubbed everything but his teeth. Sometimes I'd almost drool as I washed each of his gnarled fingers, remember the nights. When I got to "down there," he'd pretend he didn't notice. If he'd looked, he probably would have known I was truly perverted, as I had difficulty some days letting go of "them." They were so perfectly formed, nuzzled in their nest of thick black curly fur. Plump.

"I'm really tired," Brook said as I bent over and hugged him. "I've got an awful headache." I couldn't let go of his head. I wanted to let go of it. "Please, Lewis. Don't!" I said nothing, just started licking his face, nibbling on his face and neck. Tears dribbled out as I held on to his head.

"Two months, Brook, I've waited two months," I mumbled. How I wanted to satisfy my desire to throw back those mounds of covers that protected him from me, grab that awful yellow rubber urinal, and rip it off. I wanted to touch him. I decided to touch him. No more lying there teasing me. No, sir! Washing "down there," as he called it, had become agonizing for me. Holding it, kneading it clean to lock up in that rubber cell. "Oasis used to melt into me." He had described her melting into him. I saw her melting into him. Tommie melting into him as I held on to him. "Lewis, stop it!" he commanded. "You are embarrassing me. Yourself. Can't you see I don't want this?" He sounded so far away. I tried to enter his mouth. He tightened his jaws. I kissed him on his eyelids. He opened his eyes as wide as he could to hide them from me. I slung his covers back anyway and climbed on top of him, placing my mound smack on top of that contraption. Then I began to try to melt into him, rhythmically grinding, trying to melt into that rubber. Something, perhaps pity, maybe fear, forced him to submit to me. He relaxed and began to respond. I burrowed my nipples into him as I swayed. He began to help.

"I'm here. Go on. Let it go. I'm so sorry. What have I done to you?" he asked in a whisper that cracked. I took his nose. He gave me his mouth as it began to descend.

For a long time I lay on his left side with my eyes closed, trying not to breathe. I was so miserably ashamed of my deed.

"You've got to pull yourself together. Tommie is due here . . . typing . . . you know, it's Friday." I managed not to look at him as I untangled myself. I felt thick, old, as I propelled myself out of his bedroom.

"Can you help me get up in the morning, Lewis?" I heard him ask quietly.

"You bet!" I said very loudly, sitting down on the seat and sobbing silently.

Self-centered witch, do you really think that you are the first woman that ever did anything for me? Loved me? Wanted me? How do you think I made it before I met you? I've had lots of volunteers over twenty years, both sexes, all races, at least fifty different nationalities. Don't you think I know that most of you would rather help me than live your own frustrated lives? Unlike most men, I can't kick an ass. I can't walk out of a room when I get ready. I only rarely can select whom I want to touch me. Bunches of you have walked through this very apartment. 'Our little sanctuary,'" he mimicked. "You love the sense of power it gives you. You love being made to give, period. I inspire you to work

harder. Little old ladies used to pat my head and tell me
what an inspiration I was to them. They loved to grab my
head and hold it to their breasts, too. Just like you. Get
out of here, Lewis! You say I make you feel like a servant.
I don't have that power. You say I abuse you. I'm sick of
that phrase. I am abused, too, by women who demand
entertainment, who won't go home and leave me alone.
I'm tired of trying to figure out whose period is when
just so I'll be able to get bathed without unpleasantness.
You are the worst of all, however," he declared, lock-
ing his eyes to mine. "At least the others I've inspired,
and abused, and manipulated don't stink up my house
with foul language, liquor, and cigarettes. They do stop
talking sometimes. And they don't demand that I know
everything about them. You think everything about you
is important to everyone else—especially me. You suck,
Lewis. You really do. You pimp Woody. You dissect Gus
as if he's a fish. Prince stories are used to entertain everyone. The only one you even appear to respect is Kitty.
And that's because you two are so much alike—haughty
bitches. I am tired of trying to pay the price for our relationship. It's not worth it. The gifts, the experiences, the
fun, the good care, take them and disappear. Go back
underneath that rock you must have crawled out from
under. You price is too high!" he screamed out, dropping
his eyes, crying. "Your price is too high," he whispered,

exhausted. I went into the bathroom, got over the toilet, retched, and then threw up until the hurt stopped.

"Lewis," he called from outside of the door. "Lewis, I apologize. Come on out. Come on, let me rub your back. I know you're tired, too. Want some Bols Apricot Brandy and vanilla ice cream? A back rub? Lewis, you're the one who claims to believe most in freedom of expression. Come on out," he pleaded.

Getting up off that cold tile floor, I felt as if I weighed a thousand pounds. Stopping at the mirror, I peeped in only to see an aging clown. I remembered somehow what the others had said I should remember. "Just imagine not being able to get out of bed by yourself, baby. That can make anyone angry," Woody had said.

"Lewis, I saw the dude put his dukes up when he saw me walk into this room. He was thinking he'd rather read about folks like me than meet us. He's a fighter. I dug the way he threw his board aside as we talked. He didn't want Prince to see him leaning on nothing."

"He's an intellectual and a gentleman. I'm sure you'll try to reduce him," Augus had said.

"I love you, Lewis, for loving him so. He's handsome, charming, and witty, babe. But chile, the boy has a big brain left if little else," Kitty said.

"I apologize, too," I said, slowly opening the door. "I'll take you up on the treats. I am tired."

'm not a territory to be possessed by squatters like you." I heard him more clearly than I did the alarm clock that morning. I heard myself, too, right after he finished. "You don't like how I conduct my train, Lewis? Then hop off. Now!" The sigh that followed was still clear enough to me to break a crystal vase. I heard me ranting. "Crippled son of a bitch. I wish that man had wrung your neck completely off!" I trembled, remembering staring at those coffee spots on his kitchen ceiling, the ones left from that time he slung hot coffee at his wife. Automatically I'd unplugged the hot water urn and placed it into the sink, where he couldn't reach it. He'd sat pulling on his fingers, wishing he could rise and crush me.

"I *am* crazy. Why else would I be with you? You're right! You're not a territory. You're a leech."

One day as I drove him to his driving class at the rehabilitation institute, Brook educated me about hospitals. "At first, after my injury, I wanted to die. There I was, all six feet five inches strapped down to this hospital bed, even my head. Nothing was moving but my eyeballs, Jack. My mother was standing at the foot of the bed, crying softly. She'd lost weight in her face. For the first time she looked old to me. My injury weakened her physically and emotionally, maybe killed her," he said softly, unthinking. "I decided right then to never let her know I felt all stretched out, tied down and trussed up that way. Her Sonny."

"What'd you say to her first?" I kept my eyes focused on Mack Avenue and the traffic, feeling that Brook was crying as he remembered. He was the one man I never wanted to make cry.

"Nothing. All I could do was roll my eyeballs. So I crossed them for her until she realized I was clowning and started smiling. My father was the first one to hear me speak. I think I managed to get out 'Papa.' They took me to rehabilitation after I came home just like you're doing. My mother always got very depressed, too, on the mornings we had to go, until I explained away her fears. This depress you?" he asked as I drove up to the door.

"No," I lied, hoping to muster the energy to get his chair reassembled and him out of the car for the second time within ten minutes.

"There is laughter. And romance within these walls. Life inside is not as bizarre as it might appear. This is a little city," he said as I got out. "There are tears, confusion. Lots of laughter." He had a way of sitting as he waited for me to assemble his chair that reminded me of a general reviewing his troops.

"I had two love affairs during my year's stay in the hospital," he said as I opened up the car door. "I wouldn't have survived without the . . ." He was searching.

"Special attention?" I contributed, placing his board under his behind.

"That's it. Right. One was a Japanese doctor. She had soft brown eyes, just about five feet tall. The other was a

Frenchwoman volunteer that came every Wednesday." I grabbed him by his thick black leather belt in preparation for helping him slide across his flying board onto his chair. He automatically anchored his right hand onto the roof of my car. As he began to synchronize our movements by counting one, two, three, I again questioned God in silence about his decision for Brook. If I weren't afraid of Him, I would have cursed Him as I rehearsed Brook's lifetime sentence: "Anesthetize him from the shoulders down. Now! Forever."

"Can you imagine what it's like to have someone else perform the basic life functions for you?" I was straightening his pants legs.

"Not beyond give me some money."

"Those two women helped me to understand that manhood is more than straddling a woman or fathering children. Thanks," he said as I placed his board across the arms of his chair. He always said "Thanks." "They shared their minds."

"Just their minds?" I asked jokingly, pushing him toward the center door.

"Sometimes their lunches," he added with a laugh.

Brook insisted upon waiting for Tommie one evening outside of her Christmas job at this department store. I'll never forget how his voice quivered in excitement when he saw her coming through the revolving door.

"Mr. Fields!" she exclaimed in a surprised voice when she saw us.

"Hi, Tommie. We were down here shopping. Lewis thought you might like to have dinner with us. Mrs. Richards made peanut butter chicken." I was wondering how much money he could collect if he sat outside this same store, banging a tin cup of pencils on his board. Show fare?

"Can't," she responded, crinkling up her nose the

way I hated when she talked. He looked as if he wanted to lick the freckles off her nose. "Going roller-skating," she explained. "There's my date." She pointed to a young man patiently waiting in a steel-gray Jaguar. "See you after work on Friday," she said, trotting quickly toward that car.

Valium- and alcohol-saturated, I lay in Woody's bed and imagined all kinds of things. I imagined Woody wanted me there. I imagined I couldn't get out of bed without his help. Yesterday he'd even washed my feet, which I imagined were caked with mud. I imagined Brook and Tommie making love. I imagined them talking about me. "Tommie, honey, please hurry up and finish me," he said, placing the telephone on the hook. Tommie was scrubbing between his legs, staring at his beautiful boy all snuggled in between his thighs. "I don't want you here when she comes. She's quite mad, you know. She says she's coming over right now."

"She got a key?" she asked, drying him out.

"Of course not. You're the only friend that's got a key."

"Can she walk through a steel door?"

"She just might. Hurry, okay?" I could hear the excitement in his voice.

"Who told you she was mad?" she asked, powdering him.

"She did!" He was watching her calmly strap his rubber leg urinal onto his right calf.

I saw her sliding on a fresh pair of starched jeans. His shoeless six feet of legs limply sprawled across the horseshoe she had made of her own short thighs. I wanted to slap her when I heard her coyly comment in that elfin voice as she zipped his fly, "Dr. Fields, you're always talking about how important balance is in your life. Why do you select unbalanced women as friends?" I caught his silence, saw him flush red. Coughing nervously as she fastened on his suspenders, I was sure he'd repeated, "Please hurry up, honey. She'll be here soon."

And I knew she'd say, "I'm gonna stay," as she pulled him up from his pillows by his wrists.

S he's quite mad," he said to Tommie before she could get the phone back on the cradle.

"He just told that little bitch that I'm quite mad," I relayed to Woody. He was lying quietly beside me with his eyes closed. I knew he was awake because he was carefully holding a Moosehead beer bottle on his stomach. Nuzzling in on him like a newborn pup does his mother, I continued, "Am I crazy, Woody? I can't tell anymore. I'm the same me I've always known."

"You're not crazy to me. You're daring. Most people cannot even imagine life the way you live it."

"Am I mad for loving him?" I asked, reaching for my vial of blue Valiums stashed under my pillow.

"You're wonderful for loving him," he responded, placing that Moosehead on the floor. "Rest, baby," he instructed, watching me swallow three of my dolls.

All her mother asked, after I demanded that she keep Tommie away from Brook because I intended to marry him, was this one question: "How does he do it? With his mouth?"

"His mind!" I added, hanging up on her.

"I didn't do it," I lied quite calmly over the telephone.

"They said you did," he retorted. I imagined him sitting very erect in his chair, staring at the telephone's cradle and wishing it was my head so he could crush it with his jaws. "I'm tired of your absurd behavior. I dare you to have called and told her mother those lies. Tommie is not in my way. In fact, she has done more for me that I needed than you ever could. You do not intend to marry me, as you told her; you intend to kill me. How can you take care of me when you cannot stay sober enough to take care of yourself? What ghastly nerve you have. You're a witch."

I looked around my icy-blue bedroom for something to hold on to. Woody peeped in that very moment to wave a kiss goodbye.

"You have put it into that bulletproof head of yours that you are my woman. You are not! I need all the assistance I can get. I thought you understood."

"Brook?" Woody asked with a boyish smile.

I nodded yes.

"Tell him he's living the life I'd like to live. Got my favorite woman crying her heart out over him, begging to cuddle him."

Gently, Woody caressed my swollen face with his fingertips, held me. I guess Brook overheard Woody because that's when he slammed the cradle up on his end.

They unlocked the door after he ate the breakfast she had cooked while I waited outside in the hallway. As I stepped forward, she braced herself against the back of his chair, prepared to push him forward at his word. She was visibly angry at me. I saw this in the way her thick eyebrows were lifted. Brook sat erectly in his chair, trying to look at least five feet high. He was angry and frightened. "We're on our way out. May we get by?" he asked. She stared forward.

"Certainly." I moved inside, not back as they planned. I didn't stop until I reached his living room windows. I wanted to walk right through them. "I'll wait." She pushed him through that door, slamming it.

"Show of strength," Sestra said slowly. "Be careful, little sister, don't bring her boy out."

I could almost hear him repeat his little story. "She's really nuts, honey. I want you out of this. She'll cool out. I'll cool her out."

I stood at that window, watching until she pushed him out of my view. She moved that chair as if she were crossing the stage at the Barrymore with a flower cart. Her ballerina stance made me feel all lumpy. I ran into the bathroom and let go of the end of yesterday's breakfast. Out of pure spite, I used his toothbrush. "He's only a neck and a head, girl," I said to my image in the mirror. "He's mean. He's been using your kindness." The reflection staring back looked exactly like my grandmother.

Coming out of his bathroom, I smiled at the neatly folded blanket and pillow on his couch. I was sure I smelled her on my side of the bed. I turned and walked into his bedroom. Streaks of baby powder for protecting his skin crisscrossed his bed. I'd really unnerved her. Usually I could not tell exactly when she'd been there. Without him present, his room seemed cloudy, colorless, cluttered. Greasy fingerprints marred his wall calendar in the daylight. His old blue terry cloth robe that I had worn many a predawn morning rested limply on the back of an old chair. I wondered how she looked in it. He'd jokingly said I looked like a prizefighter. Reaching down beneath his bed, I pulled out her cheap cotton slides, pulled off the rosebuds, threw them onto his pillow, and returned them to their place. "Get out of here, sister," Sestra blew into my ear. "Now! He had to suck you in order to continue living. He had no choice."

"You mean he's a vampire?" I asked her.

"Sort of," she responded, "by accident. He feels he has many reasons to live. You seem to have forgotten yours," Sestra screamed within me. "Love yourself, sister."

I waited, lying defiantly on his flotation pillow. When I heard the door open, I turned my back so that we would not have to look at each other. I heard her leave him at the hall door. "Why are you humiliating us this way?" he asked very quietly as he slowly rolled up to his bedroom door. "I have asked you out of my life. You don't respect my life. Or yours. You are an embarrassment to me. I don't love you." But you do need me, I thought, tightening my eyes.

"You think I'm crazy. What sane woman could love a man who turns his back on her only hours after she helped him to turn over? When I let you use my limbs, of course I get tired." The tears returned.

"Will you please go, Lewis?"

"I can't!" I replied, rolling over. "I want to," I said as I got up and headed for my bottle in his refrigerator.

"Please don't!" he yelled after me. "It is not Tommie. It is you who's causing the loss," he yelled out as I reached the refrigerator.

A room looks different when you wake up on its floor. This one was silent except for his typing. His typing was no minor miracle, considering the fact that he typed from his neck. My cheeks were burning slightly from the scratchy rug. Buried within my left armpit was an empty fifth of vodka. I almost smiled, thinking what I must have looked like, before I realized I was lying on his floor, uncovered, in my own vomit. My eyes must have been slits. "The crippled mother let you lie here in your own puke." I forgave him for the lack of cover when I remembered how difficult it would be for him to reach a blanket. "Drunken old has-been" marched from one ear to the other across my skull in neon lights, mostly red.

"Get out of my home and my life," he'd yelled. "I have no passion for you."

"But you have a need." I saw myself pull his chair back from his door each time he tried to leave that room. I heard him scream for help again.

"Aging, pill-popping parasite bitch. Why should I need you? You can't do whatever you please to me!" He'd thrown his head back and shaken it until his torrents of tears had stopped flowing. "That alcohol you force-feed your body has stuffed up your pipes forever. It comes out of your mouth, your ass, and your pores now. The only sign you're missing is a puffy red nose, my dear," he had continued as I walked into the kitchen and slowly took my fifth out of the freezer. "Those two stomachs will turn into three by spring," he promised as I returned with it up to my mouth. "That's it, girlie, do it in front of me. I've heard you sneaking slurps for months. Spread your ass some more, Chickadee. Pretty soon it'll be riding your knees. You're an insult. Chug-a-lug. Go on," he'd said, staring at me. "Yep, I'm mean. Selfish. Why shouldn't I be?"

I'd turned that bottle up and sucked like there was no bottom. "My brain is not paralyzed, Lewis," he'd said softly. "Yours is, however. And not accidentally."

That stuff seemed to shoot right through me. I think I wet my panties a little as it took over my body. "Please leave. I don't need your kind of help. Your price is too high." Slowly I descended to his floor. "I like softness, manners."

"Ladies," I squeezed out as I sank.

"I am not a territory to be occupied by squatters. You

don't like how I conduct my train? Then jump off. Now!"
He'd wheeled himself over to me. I was glad he couldn't
kick me.

After I got up, I went behind his armchair and pulled
out Tommie's birthday gifts. I'd selected them: two real
satin teddies, navy and beige lace, sea green and beige
lace; a box of black sheer stockings. The scissors waited
in the shopping bag with the wrappings and ribbons. I
picked them up to use on her gifts. How funny it would
be to see her face after she opened up those pretty gold
boxes and found those beautiful teddies cut in half. I
ended up in his study with those scissors. He didn't look
at me until I got real close to him. I saw his raw terror.
I lifted those black stockings up in the air and draped
them over his head. The pieces looked like streams of
smoke descending. I tried to stuff one into his mouth.
Then I cut holes in the teddies where their button breasts
were placed. Brook didn't say a word, just sat there rig-
idly. When I finished, he turned, tried to get his telephone off its cradle without taking his eyes off me. As
he searched for the 9, I went out like a set of Christmas
tree lights. His cries for help sounded so far from us. The
blood and the gash in his neck, his arm lifted to protect
his head.

"Boys got hard, hard heads," Sestra whispered.

EPILOGUE

Woody! Woo-dy! Wood-dee! My voice cried out to my ears as I crashed through his bedroom door. I'd driven eighty miles an hour, run every red light between Brook's and Woody's. I smirked thinking about them trying to decide whether to give me a speeding ticket or life.

"Hi, Lewis," two voices chanted right before I flipped on the light. They were trying to unfold their bodies quickly before I reached his bed. Cookie looked like a girl looks when her mother catches her in bed with the neighborhood's bad boy. Woody looked like he knew my next move.

"Hi," he repeated. "Thought you were staying at

Brook's tonight." He was trying to get out of bed and reach for his drawers on the floor at the same time. They were the droopy blues I hated. Cookie stood up, wrapped up in the sheet. They must have smelled the fury on me. "What's that on you, baby?"

She tried to ease by me but I was too fast. I got her right between the eyes with my fist the second before he got to us.

"Run along, Cookie," he instructed her. "Wait in Rose's room!" He sounded so professional. "How'd you mess up your pretty dress?" His voice was a long way away, like he was at the bottom of a valley talking up at me.

"Him," I heard myself say.

"Brook?"

"Brook," I hissed. My throat hurt. "You protecting your whore bitch?" I got out as I slammed him in the face with my fists. "You snot-eating bitch." At this he grabbed me, throwing me down. "Trying to kill me. You're trying to kill me," I screamed out as he forced me onto his bed. I remember thinking I smelled a rotten scent flowing from between my legs.

"What did you do, Aunt Lou?"

"I paralyzed his head." I felt thick spit forming in my mouth.

"Brook's?"

"Brook's," I mimicked him. "Let me up, freak fag-got!" I felt cold.

"Rest, Lewis. I'll be right back," he promised, bundling me up in his blanket. "Sleep," he whispered, wiping the sweat from my face.

Daddy's big baby, I remember thinking as my eyes and ears abandoned me.

"I'm really sorry. I always think that things will turn out right. It's becoming a weakness of mine." Woody's voice cracked as he talked to his ceiling, trying to avoid me and my makeup and my eyes. He was lying shirtless on the top of his antique bed. I was naked except for my costume. The logs in his fireplace crackled as he tried to speak. I felt light. I felt high, as I silently watched him from the other side of his spacious bedroom. John Blair crooned over his sitar in the background, *"Sometimes when a man loves a woman."*

The only light in the room outside of the fire came from the one track light Woody had left screwed on. For some reason he usually used only one light out of the eight. This one was dimmed. I'd dimmed it. I wanted to yank off his things and throw them in the fire, watch 'em burn, smell 'em. The chair I reclined in was brown leather and shiny chrome. Woody's chair. White lavender-scented talcum powder clung to the cherry-red and teal-blue designs I had drawn on my body. I'd painted blue lips and cherry-red eyes. Most of my hair was now on the floor surrounding his chair. Could he see the fury now?

"What can I do for you, Lewis?" He asked this as he got up to turn that record off.

"Crawl inside," I spat out, sprawling my legs open, showing him with my second finger where.

"What else?"

"Die! Now!"

"Can't do that, Lewis. I can't die for you. That's the one thing I cannot do for you, baby," he said as he took his pants off and got back onto his bed. "I honestly thought I was helping you."

"Helping?" I was still inside myself, probing. He was looking at me now.

"Yes."

"You fuck!" I screamed out at him, spreading my legs farther. "You gave me away. Remember that time you watched Kitty and Robb fuck me?"

"Yes."

"Even then?" I screamed.

"Yes!" he screamed back. "It was beautiful. You all loved each other," he reasoned.

"You didn't give me any babies." My voice sounded small.

"You never requested any," he responded.

"You got into my dreams and changed them into fantasies," I shouted at him. "You attacked them until I have none left."

"I gave you reality." His voice broke on this. The first tears came. "Baby, I didn't know."

"You never loved me." I slowly took my finger from within my tunnel and placed it into my mouth.

"I love you too much. I thought the way to love you was to allow you to remain free to experience life as you wished to do it." The tears flowed down his hairy chest now. I took my finger out of my mouth, placing it squarely on my little girl. She was marbleized.

"Freedom to destroy myself . . ."

"Freedom to love yourself, Lewis. To love anyone you chose."

For a minute I started to get up and go into his closet, get his genuine black leather belt with the abalone shell buckle, and do what Augus had suggested I do: "Select his largest belt, one with a large buckle, baby. Make him get down on all fours and give it to him. Spank him until the leather cracks or he comes. Then you make the most tender love to him, baby. Fuck him and his mind."

"I oughta beat your ass," I said, really getting into my little girl. I could feel her begin to tighten up in response to my caresses.

"You already have, Lewis." He sounded like an eighteen-year-old virgin from Muncie, Indiana. "Fuck his mind," Sestra screamed out at me. I rose and slowly walked over to the bed, climbed across his neck, and squatted so that he could touch her if he chose.

Mrs. Annie Simmons went berserk one day, walked down our street butt-naked. I was coming home from school. They threw her down on the sidewalk. She kept yelling out, "Help me, Jesus. Somebody help me. They're trying to kill me." Mr. Simmons threw his blanket over her and held her down and waited for the policemen. Spit foamed at the corners of her mouth as she quieted and stared straight up at the sky.

LOOK BACK BUT DO NOT STARE

Afterword by Nettie Jones

What inspired me to write *Fish Tales*? Insufficient funds! I needed to support myself. My life had dried up. We're talking about someone who had been married twice, had a child at seventeen, and was trying to live something like a normal life. Writing was a way out of my predicament.

I had made a deal with my second husband. He was a dentist and he wanted to expand his practice by becoming an orthodontist. "Okay, I'll help you do that." Recognize that? That's the voice of a young wife who hasn't yet learned to get hers first. Later on, I decided it was time for him to pay me back: when he finished becoming an orthodontist, I could finish becoming who I wanted to be, which was free.

In 1972, when I was thirty-one, I left Detroit for New York, to attend the New School for Social Research to earn a second master's degree, this time in anthropology and sociology. It was also a polite escape from my troubled marriage. Cocktail hour started at five o'clock every day; I added Valium, prescribed to me by a bevy of psychiatrists to treat my manic depression. Our sexual preferences were incompatible, which led to adultery, although I always believed he was innocent; there was proof of our love in our home, our sailing yacht, our cars, or so I thought. Separating seemed like the solution, and it was, for a while.

I became mesmerized by life in Chelsea and Greenwich Village, by the people I met, the streets. I shared an apartment in the West Village with a psychiatrist who worked at Harlem Hospital. For the first time in my life, I walked as a woman alone. Eventually I got caught up with unsavory persons, dangerous characters who fascinated me, but who repelled so-called "normal" human beings, some of whom eventually became the characters in *Fish Tales*.

During one of my rages, I moved back to Detroit to live again with my second husband and my daughter, Lynne. I did not like to think of the consequences of my time away.

In 1977, I met a scholarly gentleman in Detroit.

Within about forty-eight hours of meeting him, I was totally infatuated. He was quadriplegic, and where I may have expected to see just some guy in a wheelchair, I saw this beautiful man, six-foot-five—and those eyes! He asked me what I did; I knew I had to say something to really wow him. I couldn't tell him I was just having a good time. So I told him I was writing a book. It's true that I'd been doing some writing while I was in New York—something the psychiatrist suggested, by the way, so I'd have something to do other than shopping. But I'd burned it all, all fifty pages of it, in my fireplace in New York.

And in his very refined Southern accent, he comes back with, "Do you want to write a book? Or do you want to be a writer?"

"I want to be a writer."

My reading at the time was dictated by classroom requirements. I was so tired of reading about all these tragic stories, books by too many women writers, SAMO SAMO SAMO! Just like Basquiat graffitied all over New York. I wanted to go forward. I was reading Iceberg Slim, books like *Dopefiend*, and magazines like *Hustler* and *Playboy*; I was reading *The Advocate*. He told me that I should meet this young woman writer at the University of Michigan, Gayl Jones.

Gayl had gone to work at Michigan with an offer of

full tenure. She had two acclaimed books, *Corregidora* and *Eva's Man*. All this by her midtwenties. I got an appointment with her and drove to Ann Arbor. I had my journals—my husband had given me a pile of green leather books with gilt-edged pages. I left them with Gayl to read, and after a month or two we met again. This time I asked her, "Should I be a writer?"

Slightly above a whisper, she spoke one word: "Write." No expression, no smile.

She never showed me how to write—she was a critic, a historian—but she knew when she looked at me what I needed to read. She gave me two books, *Everything and Nothing*, by Dorothy Dandridge, the first Black female actress to be nominated for an Oscar, and *Play It as It Lays*, by Joan Didion. She gave me a list of editors and agents. Two or three of them rejected me. Another of them was Toni Morrison, who accepted *Fish Tales* readily.

While I was writing the book, I lived in a little town called Leland, on the Leelanau Peninsula, about 250 miles from Detroit, on Lake Michigan. The summer homes of some of the wealthiest people in the country were right next door. The Ball Mason jar people were nearby, and Oscar Mayer's son owned a golf club and a little restaurant. Pristine people in pristine country.

Guess what? It was wonderful! It was paradise. Jim Harrison was around, along with a few other writers. I was writing in a valley of wildflowers, in a house built by the young man who sold it to me. A few little acres came with it. I would do my writing in my lovely little house, outside at the picnic table beneath the pine tree, or at the sand dunes. I was in a writer's dream world. It was picturesque, and I was doing just what I was supposed to be doing. I wrote *Fish Tales* as it came to me, through my senses. I heard it, I felt it move through my body, all the way to my fingertips, holding on to a Blackwing pencil. I wrote it the only way I know how: to dramatize the truth, to make people greater than they are—more grotesque, immoral, untamed. Or, are they just people we didn't used to accept as good folk? It was about men I had known, mostly—and I'd known a few.

When the book came out, it was 1984. How thrilling is it to see yourself in the *New York Times Sunday Magazine*? How exciting is it to see yourself in the Wednesday *New York Times*? You can get uppity.

Around then I was at Yaddo, working on my second book, *Mischief Makers*. While I was there a few of the other writers were getting positions at their colleges and universities, so I wrote to the humanities department at

Wayne State University and told them they should hire
me as a writer in residence—I was a graduate of their
school, I had taught nine years in the Detroit Public
Schools system, and I was a citizen of their city—and
they did. I was trying to figure out how to afford my lust
to be a writer. My advance for *Fish Tales* was $3,000, not
enough to replenish the fortune it took to create. *Mischief Makers* was published in 1989. I got $3,000 for that
one, too.

When that residency was ending, I told them I
wanted to stay. There was more work to be done. Besides,
there were these people, mostly white folks, coming in to
do their single semester, flying in from Paris or whatever,
and their offices stayed empty and open for them all year
round. "You see all these white people coming in? You
gotta get me something too." So they gave me a couple
classes to teach in Grosse Pointe.

By this time, I had financially broken myself and my
second husband, who was the inspiration for Woody in
Fish Tales. He told me he didn't own my body. But between his dreams and mine, my second husband and I
had washed out. The sailboat, the house in Detroit, the
one on the peninsula—we were living fantastically, but
who was going to pay the bills for all this dreaming?
Many marriages are not held together by anything more

than paychecks or children, but people like to pretend there's more there.

In 1988, I met Gloria Naylor. She helped get me a writer-in-residence position at Michigan Tech University, so I left Detroit. I taught and brought visiting writers to Michigan Tech. I had a class and did community work. I got people jobs. I ran an event called Tech Take Three. Every Wednesday I put on an event featuring either a faculty member or a guest I'd brought in—musicians, politicians, scholars—and I'd serve tea and crumpets. I received support to invite Mother Rosa Parks to the 1989 commencement, where she received an honorary doctorate. My highest honor to this day was to welcome her to the university.

Eventually, it was time for me to go. It was a wandering life. It seemed like when the time came to leave a place, I'd go somewhere new where I could learn and teach. I did some of everything I could to sustain myself.

I thought I'd go to the University of Chicago Divinity School. My daughter was living in Chicago and wanted me to come to her, but before I left, she came to visit me and didn't want to leave, so she stayed up there and I went to Chicago. I met scholars of Eastern and

Western religions, theologians. I lived among nuns and Jesuit priests—now, *that* had an effect on me.

Then I met the writer Glenda Taylor. At times she and her family took me in when I needed a place to stay. The last time, I'd come back from Jamaica after I'd left a position at the Gallatin School at New York University. I had given up everything to go to Jamaica, but my health went bad there so I had to give that up, too. I had no place else to stay. Glenda helped me find a room in the Lenox Hill Women's Mental Health Shelter, for women forty-five and older. Glenda had run several nonprofits, and she knew what to do; she'd already written to the mayor, the governor, to tell them I was a national treasure and I was homeless, and what were they going to do about it? She told me, "You'll only be there two to three weeks," but I was there for fifteen months waiting for space to open up.

That was grand living, on Park Avenue, about two blocks from Central Park. People have negative ideas about shelters, but they're not all bad, though they need more public support. There were a lot of people you wouldn't expect to find in places like that: nurses, teachers, businesspeople who'd suffered, had mental, physical, spiritual problems. Then you add the drugs to it, and the loss of any status they'd once accumulated. We were all different kinds of people. One woman, just out of prison, came in selling items she'd lifted. She couldn't do without the drugs. Overdosed in the bathroom and died.

If someone said they didn't like me, I learned how to get up in their face and say, "Well, what you gonna do? I've lived a long time and I ain't got nothing to lose." Tough talk.

I learned there was work to do: What could we do to make homelessness better understood? I started a group with two women, one named Evelyn, the other Debbie. We called it the Daisy Society. Everyone would ask questions. I would read. Glenda helped; she sent homemade cakes and she arranged for well-known people to call in to talk to us. We were hooked up to the telephone, sitting around the table. Those of us who had an income, Social Security benefits, bought all the fresh fruit and desserts we could eat. We talked to them about voting, their grandchildren—and many of these women, in their forties, did have grandchildren.

I've spent my life learning about other people. You can almost instantly know the ones who you can work with and the ones who can work with you. I would talk to the guards, the security, the desk people. I was always asking, "What can we do to make this better?"

I'd like to go back to that valley of flowers someday. I'd take some of the women I've met in this life with me. We'd get some dogs, cats, and a peacock. We'd get a little rest from life in the big city.

Writers fight in our own ways. In the end it has something to do with accepting life as it unfolds, accepting other people. It means understanding that it is our task to do good unto each other. My protection has been the courage and gifts given to me by my God. I tried to make sure that I made some history while on this earth. And I did.

ACKNOWLEDGMENTS

First and foremost, my deepest thanks
to Marie D. Brown. And thank you to:

Lavern Bostic
L. Todd Duncan
Michael Gonzales
Frank W. Harris
Naomi Huffman
Jenna Johnson
Gayl Jones
Louis Jones
Valerie Jean Kindle
Fern Logan
Toni Morrison
Bonnie L. Rattner
Julia Ringo
Carl Taylor
Glenda R. Taylor

A Note About the Author

Nettie Jones is the recipient of a National Endowment for the Arts Individual Artist Award, a Yaddo Foundation fellowship, a Michigan Council for the Arts grant, a New York University Gallatin School of Individualized Study Student Choice Award, and a Carnegie Fund for Authors grant. *Fish Tales*, her debut novel, was first acquired by Toni Morrison, who was then an editor at Random House, and it was originally published in 1984. *The New York Times* named Jones a promising new novelist in 1985. Her second novel, *Mischief Makers*, was published in 1989. Her essays and short stories have appeared in numerous magazines and anthologies.